I0611220

Other Titles by Milton Stern

The Girls (1985)

America's Bachelor President
and the First Lady (2004)

Harriet Lane, America's First Lady (2005)

On Tuesdays, They Played Mah Jongg (2006)

Michael's Secrets (2009)

MEN, MUSCLE & MAYHEM

AN EROTIC COLLECTION BY

Milton Stern

Herndon, VA

Copyright © 2011 by STARbooks Press

First Edition

ISBN 10: 1-934187-84-4

ISBN 13: 978-1-934187-84-5

This book is a work of fiction. Names, characters, places, situations and incidents are the product of the author's imagination or are used fictitiously. Any resemblance to actual events, locales, or persons, living or dead, is purely coincidental. All rights reserved, including the right of reproduction in whole or in part in any form.

Published in the United States by

STARbooks Press
PO Box 711612
Herndon VA 20171

Printed in the United States

Many thanks to graphic artist John Nail for the cover design. Mr. Nail may be reached at:
tojonail@bellsouth.net.

Jose A. Dennis created the image of Kosher Man based on Mr. Stern's narrative. Mr. Dennis can be reached at gryphta@gmail.com. His Website is http://www.josedennis.com.

Dedication

To Christopher Pierce, my editor and fellow author, for his support and constructive suggestions.

For Esmeralda Stern, who finally learned that some human beings are capable of love.

The characters and events in this book are purely fictional.

None of these stories ever happened ... but they could have!

CONTENTS

FOREWORD
CHRISTOPHER
PIERCE

First, let me say what an honor it is to have been given the opportunity to edit this first collection of erotica by my friend and colleague, Milton Stern.

MEN, MUSCLE & MAYHEM is not merely a book of stories where (incredibly) hot men hook up and (spectacularly) get off. The book also acts as a field guide of sorts to that much sought-after animal – the gay muscleman. Here, we find many specimens of the species both in their natural habitat (gyms) and free ranging in some unexpected places.

MEN, MUSCLE & MAYHEM also contains quite a bit of laugh-out-loud humor. I will now be checking the skies for a glimpse of Kosher Man sailing through the clouds. *Yarmulke on!*

INTRODUCTION
MILTON STERN

To some, this may be my crossing over to the dark side, but to me, this is just an extension of my dream of becoming a well-known, published author. With the release of this book, I am not abandoning my life-long aspirations, just broadening my horizons and maybe gaining a new audience.

The way I see it, everything we do in life is for our obituaries. I might as well give them something interesting to say.

KOSHER MAN

AND

THE SHEGATZ

Mordecai was sunning himself on the roof of his building, enjoying the peace and quiet of a hot summer day. The temperature was to hit 100, but that didn't faze him, for his people always vacationed where it was hot and enjoyed humid weather as well. Build a resort on the sun, and Mordecai and his tribe would be the first to make a reservation. After forty years in the desert, they grew to love the heat. That may have been over 3,000 years ago, but Mordecai was as kosher as they came.

He knew he could enjoy the mid-day sun alone as he lay there on the chaise, wearing only a dark blue Speedo that barely concealed his more than ample package, and on his head, he wore his dark blue *yarmulke* with a white *Mogen David* (Star of David) embroidered on it. No one else in his building enjoyed the heat, and in all the years he lived there, he never saw anyone come up to the roof in the summer.

Mordecai was tall, over six-foot-four, with very broad shoulders, large, naturally hairless pecs, six-pack abs, bulging biceps, and powerfully muscular legs, all covered in dark olive skin, which at the moment was glistening with olive oil. Mordecai never needed sunscreen, for he never burned. He was also known for his rather round and hugely muscular *tuchus* – buttocks to all you gentiles out there. His feet, at size 15, were not only quite large, but also magnificently beautiful.

But, it was Mordecai's face that drew people to him. He had black, curly hair that he wore short except for the top, and at over forty, his temples were graying, making him look all the more distinguished. Mordecai also had thick black eyebrows, hovering over bright green eyes framed in double rows of lashes that gave the impression he was wearing make-up, and his prominent Semitic nose led one's eyes to his full lips and gleaming white teeth. Mordecai's innocent smile could melt the coldest of hearts and made all the *yentas* and *buhbbies* want to pinch his cheeks.

On days like this, Mordecai cherished these peaceful times alone. By day, he was a cataloguer at the Jewish History Museum in Greenburg, a popular metropolis on the East Coast that drew the cosmopolitan as well as the seedy. But, cities have a tendency to do that, and Mordecai didn't mind. However, when the sun set, Mordecai emerged from the basement at the Jewish History Museum and headed home, and at the first sign of trouble, he donned a white mask and dark blue tights with a large white circled "K" emblazoned on his chest, along with white boots and a flowing white cape to become "Kosher Man." Mordecai wanted to forgo the cape as it always got in the way, but his mother insisted, and a good Jewish boy always obeys his mother. He also wore a dark blue *yarmulke* on his head with a white circled "K" as well (it was actually the flip side of his everyday *yarmulke*). His best kept secret was how he never lost the *yarmulke* while fighting evil even though one never saw a *yarmulke* fly off an Orthodox Jew's head during a wind storm either.

But, the cape was his biggest nemesis. Often when flying, it would flap in his face, making it difficult to navigate, or he would go to punch a crook and end up tangled up in the cape instead. Whenever Mordecai experienced these mishaps, he thought of the joke:

What do you call a Jewish ballerina?

A klutz.

He thought the same applied to a Jewish superhero as well.

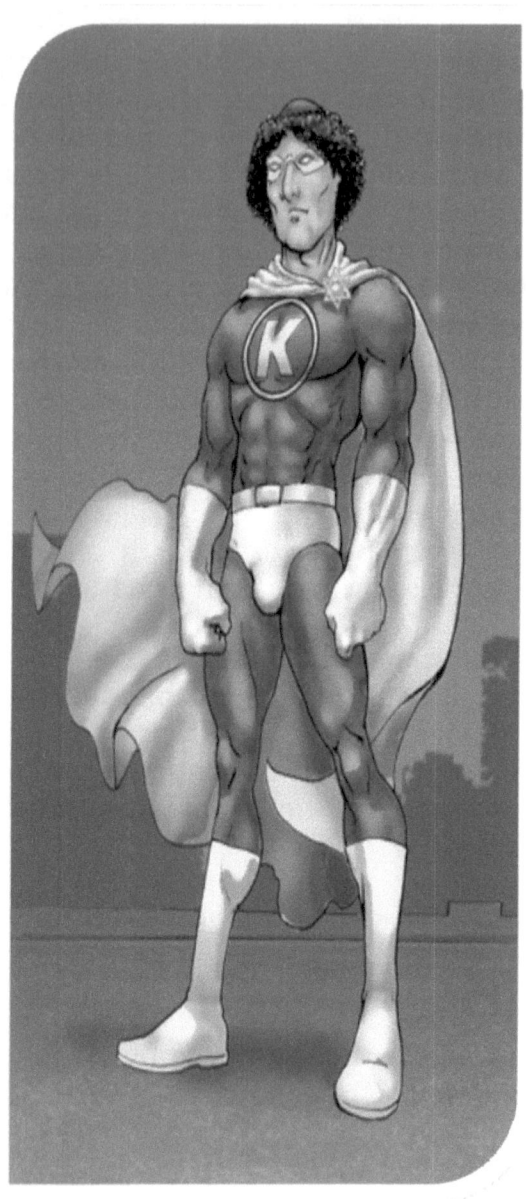

Mordecai could have lived a normal, quiet life, but he displayed special abilities from a young age. While still a toddler, he showed great feats of strength, lifting furniture and other heavy objects around the house. As he entered puberty, his body transformed without ever having lifted a weight or participated in sports. His mother insisted he read because one could get an eye poked out playing sports. In high school, coaches wanted him to play football, but participation in various geeky academic clubs precluded his lettering in any sport. Mordecai was relieved because he was aware that he sometimes did not know his own strength, and he was afraid he would more than poke someone's eye out if things got out of hand.

One day, when he was in college, he was late for class, and as he started to run across campus, he suddenly found himself airborne and gaining altitude. Startled at first, he held onto his books while extending one arm in front of himself to guide his journey, and within days, he mastered his new-found talent. Mordecai then flew home to show his mother, and she did not act surprised, for she had expected this day to come.

"When I turned forty, I knew I did not have much time left to become a mother," she told her son, after he landed in their front yard and sat beside her on the porch. "I prayed, and an angel appeared before me and told me I would have a son and this son would be very special. He would be one of the chosen ones. He would have abilities not seen for thousands of years. He would have the strength of twelve men, the wisdom of twelve rabbis, and he would soar like an eagle, yet have the heart of a dove."

Mordecai listened intently as his mother continued.

"But, the angel made me promise that no forbidden food would ever touch his lips. He would study the *Torah* and honor his parents," she said. "I was told he would have one weakness and that he also would never father children of his own."

"Why would I never father children?" Mordecai asked.

"I asked the same thing," his mother answered. "The angel told me that if I wanted a child, there were sacrifices I would have to make and mine was never to be a grandmother. I asked if you would be sterile, and the angel said it was more complicated than that. So, I pursued it no further. He then made me promise again that no forbidden food would ever pass through your lips."

"And, I have kept kosher for you, Mother," Mordecai said as he kissed her on the cheek.

Just a few months later, his mother presented him with his first getup as Mordecai referred to his tights. And ever since, he has been Kosher Man.

# # # # #

The sun was baking Mordecai, but he did not care as the heat energized him. He thought about moving to Boca or Palm Springs but figured he'd wait until retirement when perhaps another crime fighter would emerge to take his place.

Mordecai was starting to doze when he heard the yell of a man in fear. He sat up on the chaise and tried to hone in the location of the scream.

"Five blocks northwest," he said out loud. Then, Mordecai jumped from the chaise and headed for the door to the roof, opened it and disappeared down the flight of stairs to his apartment on the fourth floor. Within seconds, the window to his apartment opened, and a flash of dark blue and white flew out the window toward the northwest corner of Greenberg. Mordecai often wondered why no one ever noticed him flying out his window. But, city people were so oblivious to their own surroundings.

Once airborne, Kosher Man scanned the city, and his cape again flew in front of his face. "*Vaysmir* with this *feshtungina* cape," he cursed out loud. He swept the fabric from his face then he located the man in trouble. In an alley next to The Lost Tribe Bar, a blond man was surrounded by four men dressed in jeans and black T-shirts, which was unusual for broad daylight, even in Greenburg.

Kosher Man slowed down and slowly descended upon the scene in the alley landing almost quietly behind the four assailants, except for the metal trash can lid he knocked over with the cape. The four men turned around.

"Oh look it's the caped kike," one of them said as he pointed to Kosher Man, laughing.

"Whom are you calling a kike?" Kosher Man said as he lurched forward, grabbed the insulter by the collar and slammed him against the wall, instantly knocking him out cold.

Within seconds, like a streak of light, Kosher Man had rounded up the other three men and wrapped them up in a water hose before they realized what hit them.

"Do you have a cell phone," Kosher Man asked the blond man.

"Ye ... yes," he stammered. "Who are you?"

Over twenty years in Greenburg flying around fighting crime, and Kosher Man was surprised someone didn't know who he was. "I'm Kosher Man," he answered. It was then that Kosher Man got a good look at the man. He was in his early thirties if that old with a thick blond buzz cut, blue eyes, pale skin, but strong features. He was wearing a tight red shirt that displayed a fine physique, and he stood about five-foot ten. Kosher Man rarely went for the WASPy type, but he thought a romp with this one would be worth a few minutes of his time.

"What are you, some kind of superhero?" the man asked.

"You could say that. Now call the police before these hoodlums get loose. I have a city to patrol," Kosher Man said as he prepared for takeoff, dramatically sweeping the bane of his existence – the dreaded cape – behind him.

"Wait!" the man yelled.

Kosher Man turned back to the man and looked at his pleading gentile eyes. "What? Call the police now," the superhero asked then ordered.

"Don't you want to know my name?" the man asked.

The Hebrew hunk thought for a moment, then answered, "That's OK, kid, something tells me I'll run into you again." And with that, Kosher Man took flight.

He figured the *shegatz* (male *shicksa*) with the *goyshka* cup (gentile brain) would forget to call the police, so he swooped down on the first police car he saw, told the familiar officers what happened and where to find the criminals, and with that, he disappeared into the sky in search of more damsels – or dam-boys – in distress.

At around 4:00 am, Kosher Man zipped back into the open window of his apartment, closed the window, and with a flash, stripped off his costume, hiding it in the secret compartment in the back of his closet. He then brushed and flossed his teeth and showered in a manner of seconds and climbed into bed hoping for a good three hours of sleep.

However, Mordecai awoke two hours later with a raging boner. Spending his evenings fighting crime, with the exception of *Shabbat*, which he spent with his mother, and his days at the museum, stuck in the basement cataloguing, he rarely had a chance to go out and troll for sex.

Now, his balls were swollen, and his twelve inches (seven inches around in case you were wondering) of circumcised kosher meat with its large purple mushroom head was leaking precum like a faucet, begging for release. Mordecai ran his left hand down his muscular torso and using the abundance of precum, slicked up his dick and started stroking. It only took a few minutes before he was shooting straight for his open mouth, as he caught all he could, letting the rest drip down his chin, only to scoop it up and swallow it as well. Mordecai loved the taste of his own cum almost as much as that of the few Jewish guys he was able to pick up when he had those precious moments of free time.

He enjoyed a few more minutes basking in the afterglow and marveling at how his over-forty-year-old dick remained hard for quite a while before finally going slightly soft. Mordecai then climbed out of bed and took a long hot shower – rather than his usual supersonic one – before heading to work.

He had been in the basement for only a couple of hours, tending to his duties, when Sylvia came down, calling for him.

"Mordecai," she bellowed over row after row of books and artifacts.

"Back here," he answered, as he was looking at a piece of parchment through a magnifying glass while sitting at his desk.

Sylvia found her way back to his desk and stared at Mordecai. He was wearing loose fitting dark blue pants and a white oxford shirt that hung on his physique, being a size too large. On his head was the familiar yarmulke, and he was wearing his gray, plastic framed bifocals. (Even superheroes need reading glasses after a certain age, so when Mordecai's time came, he chose bifocals. This way he could continue wearing his disguise all the time.) Mordecai looked up at Sylvia.

"You know, Mordecai, sometimes you remind me of Clark Kent," she said with a smile.

He chuckled inside, wondering if she realized how close to reality she was with that observation.

"Anyway, Moshe called in sick," she continued. "And, I need to go to a meeting. I need you upstairs to be the guest docent for a few hours until I get back. The fresh air will do you some good."

"Now?" Mordecai asked.

"Yes," she said motioning him to get up.

Mordecai stood up from the desk and ducked his head as he worked his way through the cramped basement.

"It is amazing you have any color at all being in this basement all the time ... what has it been? twenty years?" she asked as she followed him upstairs.

"Close," Mordecai answered as he walked upstairs to the main lobby of the museum, "but I sun myself on my rooftop on the weekends."

With a flourish, Sylvia left, and Mordecai stood in the lobby looking awkward as usual. He strolled around and straightened a few of the pictures, when the door opened and a blond man walked in. Mordecai turned around and immediately recognized him – the victim from yesterday.

The man walked to the reception area, and Mordecai strolled over to greet him.

"Hi, how much to tour the museum?" he asked.

"Five dollars," Mordecai answered. The man handed him the money, and with that, Mordecai gave him a ticket and a tour.

"And that is the end of the tour," Mordecai said as he led the man back into the lobby an hour later.

"Can I ask you something?" the man asked, turning to face and look up at Mordecai. "What is your name?"

"Mordecai," he answered. "And what is yours?"

"Robert ... Robert Madison," the man answered as he extended his hand. They shook. "Can I ask you another question?"

"Sure."

"Will you have dinner with me tonight?"

Mordecai thought for a moment. In all his life, he never went on a date with a gentile. He hadn't even had sex with one. But, he figured it had been a long time since he did anything. "Sure, but we will have to eat at my mother's restaurant as I keep kosher and cannot eat forbidden foods."

"OK, where's that?" Robert asked.

"On twenty-fourth and H Streets, Mother Rose's Restaurant. I'll see you there at eight."

And with that, Mordecai had a date.

Mordecai arrived at his mother's restaurant a few minutes early. Rose had opened the restaurant soon after her husband died and Mordecai had moved to Greenburg. She knew her special son would only be able to eat strictly kosher food, and this way she could watch out for his diet without appearing to dote on him by cooking for him at his place or having him over for dinner every night.

Her eyes lit up at the sight of her only son, and at eighty-four, she was still in phenomenal shape, running her restaurant as she did the day she opened it twenty years before.

"Mordecai, shall I sit with you?"

"Actually, Mother, I have a date ... I think," he answered.

Rose looked concerned as she seated him at a booth in the back, the only one that could accommodate his large frame.

"With whom?" she asked.

"His name is Robert Madison, and I met him at the museum this afternoon," Mordecai said as the waitress placed a bowl of kosher pickles and olives on the table.

"Mordecai, you have to be careful with the *goyim*. There are plenty of nice Jewish boys out there ..."

"No, there aren't, Mother," Mordecai said. "Sometimes, I get tired of being alone. My life sometimes feels cursed ..."

"Don't you ever say that," Rose said as she sat opposite him. "Your life is blessed. You remember that ... and you be careful. A *shegatz* cannot be trusted."

"Mother, you're such a bigot," Mordecai said with a smile.

"I am not. I just think one should date his own kind," she said as she got up.

"Then I will date no one as I am one of a kind," Mordecai said, just as he spotted Robert entering the restaurant.

Robert saw Mordecai and worked his way to the back of the dining room.

"Now here he is ..."

"The blond? He looks like an Aryan," Rose said with shock.

"Mother!"

Robert walked over to the booth as Mordecai stood and introduced his mother. She nodded, handed him a menu and walked away.

Dinner went smoothly, considering everyone in the restaurant was staring at them, and Rose appeared to be studying rather than observing the two men.

Mordecai went to pay the bill, but his mother would have none of it, so he left the equivalent as the tip, and he and Robert left the restaurant.

"Where to now?" Robert asked.

"Well, I have an early day tomorrow ..."

"Don't be silly, come to my place for a drink ..."

"I don't drink," Mordecai quickly answered. "My people always eat, but rarely drink."

"Mordecai, that was my way of getting you to my apartment to have a little fun," Robert said with a smile.

"Oh," Mordecai said naïvely.

"You don't get out much, do you?"

Mordecai didn't answer as they headed to Robert's apartment.

Once inside, Robert did not waste any time. He pounced on Mordecai practically ripping off the museum cataloguer's clothes as he drove his tongue into his mouth, and Mordecai did not resist. Robert then stepped back to remove his shirt, and his eyes popped as he got the first full view of Mordecai in nothing but a pair of white briefs.

"Oh my God," Robert said as he slowly undressed himself. "Who knew that under all that baggy clothing stood an Adonis?" He removed the last stitch, and completely naked, walked over to Mordecai and ran his hands all over the superhero's body, totally unaware that he had seen that physique before, only covered in dark blue tights and wearing a white mask. As he ran his hands up the back of Mordecai's neck, he went to remove the *yarmulke,* but Mordecai stopped him.

"That stays on," Mordecai said as he grabbed Robert's wrist. Mordecai then ran his hands down Robert's furry torso and grabbed his six-inch dick, which was raging hard. Not too large, but Mordecai always marveled at smaller penises, wondering what it would be like to be normal.

Robert grabbed the waist of Mordecai's briefs and worked them down but had trouble stretching them past the tall Hebrew's hard-on.

"Here, let me help you," Mordecai said as he eased his foot-long schlong out of his briefs before sliding them down his huge thighs and kicking them away.

Robert reached for Mordecai's kosher meat with his mouth agape and his eyes wide open. "I can't get my hand around it. This is the biggest thing I've ever seen."

Mordecai eased him over to the bed, and as Robert sat on the edge of the bed facing the Hebrew sausage, he tried to get his mouth around the baseball-sized head, but it was no use.

I am cursed, Mordecai thought. But his dick was leaking so much precum that Robert worked the entire shaft and head with his tongue and lapped up every drop of the delicious nectar, moaning and leaking himself at the same time. With one hand, he stroked the length of it, and with the other, he felt every inch of Mordecai's smooth, powerful body.

Mordecai eased him on his back and worked his legs over Robert's head as he faced the *shegatz's* crotch. Six inches was fine for Mordecai, for he could get the entire length in his mouth and enjoy every drop. Robert continued doing what he could with all that cock he was given to play with – stroking and licking – and his tongue found the sweet spot between the ball sac and the asshole, marveling at how hard even that was. He reached around and ran his hands all over Mordecai's enormous muscular butt, all the while moaning in total ecstasy as his cock was deep into the hunky Hebrew's mouth. Mordecai worked Robert's cock, making it leak almost as much as his own while he rolled the gentile's pink balls in his hand. He then worked his mouth down to those balls and sucked them individually and together before working his way back to the leaking head and slurping up all that tasty non-kosher precum. Mordecai wanted to make it last, but he was so turned on by what Robert was doing to him and what he was doing to Robert that he could not hold out much longer.

With one hand on Mordecai's cock, one finger working its way into Mordecai's hole, and his tongue working back to the superhero's plum-sized balls, Robert managed to bring Mordecai over the edge. With a scream that was surely heard in all the adjacent apartments, Mordecai shot a load that splashed his own chin as he continued sucking on the gentile's cock. Spurt after spurt of his kosher spunk erupted between them before Robert also lost control and shot clear into Mordecai's mouth. Mordecai hungrily lapped up the *treyf* (non-kosher) treat and swallowed all he could.

Robert was satiated, and said, "Damn, that was hot."

But, Mordecai didn't speak. Still hovering over Robert, he started to feel a burning sensation in his gut, then he rolled off the bed onto the floor. He held his stomach and felt a pain like no other he felt before. He started to cry out, then he began to convulse to the horror of Robert who didn't know what to do.

"Oh no ... what do I do ... Oh shit," Robert whined as he went to put on his jeans and located his cell phone. He was fumbling with it, when he heard a knock at the door. With a flourish, he opened the door, and who was standing there, but Mordecai's mother.

Rose looked at Robert who was wearing only a pair of jeans that he had not had a chance to button up then saw Mordecai, naked and crying in pain and convulsing in the middle of the bedroom floor. By now, Mordecai had turned almost red as his blood was starting to boil, and he was sweating profusely. Eighty-four-year-old Rose shoved Robert out of the way and ran to her only son, the son she prayed for, the son who was a gift from God, the son who was dying right in front of her eyes.

"What did he eat?" she screamed at Robert as she knelt beside Mordecai.

Robert stood there frozen.

"What did he eat?" she screamed again. "Say something. He must have eaten something forbidden. What kind of *treyf* did you feed him? I have to know! My son is dying. What did you feed him?"

"I ... I ..." Robert stammered.

"Answer me!" she screamed as she opened her purse.

"He ... he swallowed my ...,"Robert began. "He swallowed my ..."

"*Oy vay!* Just say it. He swallowed your load. Now what did you eat today? Did you have ham? Shell fish? Bird of prey? Answer me, I need to know!" Rose screamed.

"I ... had a ham sandwich for lunch," Robert answered confused.

Rose then reached into her purse and pulled out a syringe and a vial with purple liquid in it. While Mordecai continued to convulse on the floor, she drew some of the liquid into the syringe.

"Get over here and help me hold him down. I need to plunge this into his heart," Rose bellowed.

Robert hesitated.

"Now!" she yelled as he looked right at her.

At that point, he figured she may be over eighty, but she could still probably kick his ass. Robert hurried over and helped her hold Mordecai, who although in pain and clearly dying, was still stronger than ever. He held the big man's shoulders while she aimed for his heart with the syringe of purple liquid. She may have been elderly, but her aim was perfect. The syringe went straight into his heart, and she pressed the plunger, releasing the liquid.

Within seconds, Mordecai quit convulsing. He quieted down, and his skin went from bright red to olive again. His body temperature also started to return to normal.

"Get me a blanket to cover him up," Rose said to Robert.

He pulled a blanket off the bed and handed it to Rose. She covered her son from the waist down and then pulled her cell phone out of her purse.

"I may have changed his diapers and potty trained him, and I have always known it was a large one, but I don't think he needs to wake up and find his mother staring at his naked body," Rose said as she started dialing the phone.

"What was in that syringe?" Robert asked.

"Manischewitz Concorde Grape," she answered matter-of-factly.

Rose called her friend Gert, and with Robert's help, they walked Mordecai to Rose's car – a brown Eldorado. Before she got behind the wheel, Rose said to Robert who was still in a state of shock, "I am truly sorry, but you cannot see my son again. It is a matter of life and death."

Robert did not argue; he understood. Well, he didn't really understand, but he also didn't want to witness anything like that again. He also never wanted to sleep with another Jew for fear he would accidentally kill him.

Rose spent the night at Mordecai's to be sure he was all right. The next morning, she lectured him, ending with, "Superman has Kryptonite, and you have *treyf*. If you ever eat *treyf* again, I cannot guarantee I will be there to save your life. Perhaps you should carry a Manischewitz pen."

"Yes, Mother," Mordecai said, then he kissed her on the cheek. He then looked up and cocked one ear toward the window.

With a flash and a whoosh that almost blew off her wig, all Rose saw was a dark blue and white streak go out the window followed by a crash of glass as he had forgotten to open it.

"What do you call a Jewish superhero?" she said out loud, while shaking her head and smiling, "A klutz."

A REAL GYM

Michael spent more time than he wanted on the road. When he accepted the job as a consultant for the Department of Homeland Security, he thought he would be spending his time in Washington, New York, Los Angeles and Chicago, but that was not the case. Michael found himself waking up in sleepy little towns that cartographers did not take the time to notice. Towns with names like Pungo, Kincaid, Swelterville and Destination, a town so small it was named for being a stop on a long abandoned railroad.

In an effort to ensure that the government would function in the event of a national emergency, Michael's job was to negotiate contracts for bunkers and other sites to house the country's leaders. Uncharted towns made the perfect locations for these future government facilities. The secret was negotiating a deal that did not bring attention to the sleepy hamlets. Many of the civic leaders wanted the attention and hoped to boost their economies with the government contracts. Michael, however, managed to quiet their aspirations with promises of infrastructure improvements, new schools and other necessary projects.

One Monday, Michael arrived in Erlach, Virginia, a town, located southwest of Richmond, but so small, that even the citizens of Virginia's capital had never heard of it. He was pleasantly surprised to find a motel off the main highway through town. At sixty miles per hour, one blink and the motel would have been missed; two blinks and the town would have disappeared.

Michael grabbed his bag from the trunk of his car and knocked on the office door to the Erlach Motel, which was attached to the Erlach Diner, a converted railroad dining car that held the promise of good Southern cooking that Michael always craved. No one answered the door, so Michael walked over to the diner and entered.

It was three-thirty in the afternoon, and only a couple of patrons, mostly elderly gentlemen who looked as if they had retired from a lifetime of dairy farming, were sitting at the counter. Michael sat on a stool and removed his jacket.

At forty-one, Michael looked to be in his prime. He was wearing a dark blue T-shirt and jeans. Michael loved working out, and it showed. He was six-foot-two and weighed 240 pounds. Although on the road, Michael managed to find a gym most every place he went, and when none was available, he would work out with the sixty-pound dumbbells and the push-up bars he picked up in a fitness store he stumbled upon in Swelterville. Michael's favorite exercise was push-ups. He would do a set between every exercise even when working out in a gym. If he had a couple of hours free, he would spend them doing set after set of push-ups. Michael lived for the feeling of his chest getting pumped with every rep.

He would often be in a motel room in some hick town, stripped to his briefs, sweaty and pumped from hours of push-ups. Michael would then flex in the mirror and finish his routine by rubbing out a big load from his thick cock.

One of the retired farmers took notice of Michael and stared at him. He was used to being ogled for he was a fine looking man with his olive skin, dark curly hair, thick eyebrows and lashes and dark bedroom eyes. His body was big, hairy and muscular, and Michael was often asked if he took steroids. One look at Michael's large, full balls confirmed that his physique was all natural. Michael liked to eat, and fortunately for him, everything that went into his mouth turned to muscle – everything.

The cook stepped out from the back and walked over to Michael. Michael liked what he saw. The cook was not quite as tall as Michael, but his white T-shirt and stained apron barely contained his powerful form. There was no hint of hair under his hat, and he had the face of a professional wrestler. Michael noticed the scarred forehead, which was a sure sign of self-inflicted, razor wounds to give a paying crowd the blood they craved. He judged the chef to about fifty or fifty-five, and Michael considered inviting him to his room later that night to see who could do the most push-ups for the longest time. The thought made his cock leak.

"Can I get you anything?" the cook asked.

"Actually, I wanted to get a room for few nights at the motel next door, but no one answered when I knocked," Michael said.

"That's because I'm standing right here," the cook said with a smile. He was missing at least three teeth, probably knocked out by a metal chair in some noisy arena, Michael thought.

"OK, how much is a room?" Michael asked.

"Fifty dollars a night," the cook answered, "paid in advance."

Michael leaned forward and removed his wallet, noticing the cook staring at his flexed triceps. Michael looked at the retired farmer and noticed the man had also never taken his eyes off him. He pulled $150 from his wallet and handed it to the cook while rolling his eyes in the farmer's direction.

The cook looked over at the retired farmer and back at Michael and said, "Don't mind Smitty. Every time a big, good looking guy comes into town, he wonders if he is another of my old buddies."

"From wrestling?" Michael asked.

"Yeah, how did you know?" the cook asked.

Michael motioned to his forehead and said, "You have the battle scars. I follow professional wrestling, but I cannot place you."

The cook put Michael's money in the cash register and reached under the counter, plucking out one of the keys, hooked below. He handed Michael the key and smiled.

"Remember the asshole that always wore an orange mask, wrestled dirty, and was hated by the crowd?" the cook asked.

"You're the Southern Terror?" Michael asked, and he almost shot a load in his briefs.

"The one and only," the cook said. "So, you want anything to eat before you check in?"

Michael was usually hungry, but he only ordered coffee, explaining, "I really want to work out before dinner. There wouldn't happen to be a gym in this town, would there be?"

The cook poured him a cup of coffee and said, "Believe it or not there is. It is located in the building behind the motel."

Michael put cream and sugar in his coffee, stirred it and said, "Let me guess. You own that, too."

The cook smiled again and told Michael, "As a guest in my motel, you can work out there for free. I warn you, it's just a gym, no fancy machines or prancing personal trainers, or spandexed pretty boys."

The thought of the cook's gym made Michael's cock leak again, and he said, "That's perfect. I haven't seen a real gym in years. Tell me you don't play loud bar music, and I may buy a house in this town."

"Well, you know that house across the street with a for sale sign in front?" the cook asked.

Michael laughed, wondering just how much of Erlach, Virginia, this hot, retired wrestler owned.

Michael checked into Room 24 and put his bag on the bed. He checked his messages, of which there were three from the DHS, one of which confirmed his meeting with the Mayor of Erlach the following morning at ten.

He opened his bag and pulled out his black sweat pants and an old, gray tank top. Michael was never a slave to health club fashion, so he was sure he would blend in at the cook's gym just fine.

He decided to change his underwear, since the pair he was wearing was stained with precum, not an uncommon occurrence for Michael. He never wore a jock strap, preferring the security of tight, form-fitting briefs. He slipped on his sweat pants and tank top and laced up his black Converse hi-tops. He was looking forward to walking to the building behind the motel and having a real workout. It had warmed up a bit, so Michael figured he would not need a jacket for the short walk to the gym. He also didn't bother to take a lock or gym bag, reasoning he would shower in the motel room before going to the diner for supper.

Michael stepped out of his room and made his way around back. The gym was just fifty or so feet from the motel and looked to be an old converted warehouse. Painted on the door was "S-T's Gym." Michael opened the door, and to his surprise, there were quite a few men working out. There was no foyer, only a small office to the left of the door, and two paces in, Michael found himself in the middle of a large weight room. The place was mainly lit by fluorescent light bulbs, the walls were all mirrored, and any surface that was not covered by mirrors was painted a charcoal gray.

Michael first noticed the lack of music; the only sound that could be heard was the clanking of weights and the grunting of men as they struggled against the iron. He also took in a deep breath, savoring the smell of chalk, sweat and testosterone.

As he looked around, he also noticed that most of the men were working out shirtless. No rules about decorum here. This was a real gym. His cock leaked again.

The door to the office opened, and the cook stepped out and put a hand on Michael's shoulder.

"Just like I told you, nothing fancy, but it's mine," the cook said.

Michael turned to look at him and saw that he had also changed his clothes, wearing a pair of gray sweat pants and no shirt. Even past fifty, the man was powerfully built. His shoulders were like cannonballs, and his pecs were two giant plates of muscle. Michael was jealous of the old guy's enormous traps.

"Hey, this is perfect," Michael said.

"Have a good workout," the cook said as he slapped Michael's large, round, muscular ass. It wasn't a playful slap; it was the slap of an athlete, masculine in its intent.

Michael felt his muscles pumping with blood just from standing in this gym, but he came to work out, and he was going to have a workout reminiscent of the first gym he ever joined. It was similar to this one, and he could have sworn the same shirtless muscle gods were also working out there a long time ago.

The gym was hot and humid inside with the only ventilation coming from the narrow rectangular windows located between the mirrors and the ceiling. Michael decided to forego stretching and work out like a man.

No need to warm up, he thought. *If I pull a muscle, I'll just grunt and bear it.*

His only worry was that he would come during his first set. Michael was glad he was wearing tight briefs and baggy sweat pants for his dick was already getting hard.

He walked over to the bench where a couple of obvious steroid users were working out together, and before he could ask, they offered to let him work in with them.

Wow, Michael thought. *No attitude. Just work in with us.*

This place was heaven. The guys were not only big, muscular, hot and half naked, but also they were gentlemen. But of course, they were all gentlemen; they were all between forty and sixty – that perfect generation between attitude and troll.

Michael worked out harder than he had in years, working in a set with this pair of partners and that pair of partners. He benched, he pulled, he curled, he rowed, he squatted, and he lifted. A couple of the guys kidded him about how he did a set of push-ups after each exercise, but when Michael decided to remove his loose tank top before a set of dumbbell flyes, the men took notice, and a couple of them also dropped and did twenty. His hairy chest was so pumped and his big round nipples so hard that Michael could not even see his large feet when he looked down.

As it turned out, most of the guys were old friends of the cook's and retired wrestlers, too, many of them from the days of local circuits before the extreme professional wrestling of today. Although in the ring he was the Southern Terror, the cook was popular in the arena locker rooms, and when he retired to Erlach and opened the diner, the motel, and the gym, many of his former colleagues soon followed, taking up farming or just retiring and enjoying the simple life.

The weight room started to thin out after an hour, but Michael was enjoying the place so much that he decided to keep working out. Before long, the only two guys left in the weight room were Michael and the cook.

"Don't you have to go back to the diner," Michael asked him.

"We don't get busy until about seven, so my two waitresses handle the kitchen and the floor until then," the cook said. "The gym closes at six-thirty, so if you want to get in a shower, you will need to now."

"Oh, I was hoping to work out some more," Michael said.

The cook furrowed his brow and pounded Michael's pumped chest with his fist and said, "If you do another set, you are going to bust an artery. Hit the showers, we open at eleven tomorrow. You can come in then and work out for seven hours if you want."

"That's OK, I was going to shower in my room, thanks," Michael said.

The cook grabbed Michael's shoulder and said, "You will be better off showering here. The showers in the motel will barely hold you, and besides the pressure sucks. It's a dump, but it's my dump, and I wouldn't lie to you."

Michael told the cook he didn't bring a lock or a change of clothes, but the cook would have none of it. He told Michael that these guys could be trusted and just to go commando when he walked back to his room. Michael worried that if he showered with these guys, going commando in his loose sweats would cause him a great deal of embarrassment.

The cook kept his hand on his shoulder and guided him back to the locker room. Michael had no choice.

The locker room was steamier than the weight room, and Michael could hear four or five guys in the shower laughing and talking. He located an empty locker and started to untie his hi-tops. The cook stood next to him and did the same. Michael tried thinking of dead kittens and fat women with hairy vaginas in an effort to keep from getting hard, but it only semi-worked. He hoped that straight guys did not look at another guy's dick, and when he stripped off his sweats and briefs, he took a deep breath. The cook was naked at this point and grabbed two towels, throwing one to Michael.

He looked at Michael's large endowment, including his huge, hairy balls and smiled.

"Damn kid, was your father a buffalo?" the cook said. "Is there anything small on you?"

Michael blushed and wrapped the towel around his waist catching a glimpse of the cook's ample manhood in the process. He was happy the man was circumcised as he was not a fan of foreskin. Michael figured if he was going to look, he might as well enjoy the view.

He walked toward the shower, following the cook. The shower room was as old fashioned as the weight room – just a big, open, tiled room with ten shower heads. Five of the big guys, including two of the men who let Michael work in with them on the bench were showering and talking. To Michael's surprise, one of them was soaping up the other's back, and the one getting lathered was sporting a raging hard on.

Michael averted his eyes and turned on the shower next to the cook. Showering was the only thing Michael enjoyed more than push-ups, and he stood with his hands on the tiles and let the water cascade from his head down his back. He enjoyed the feeling for quite a while. Lost in the warmth of the spray, Michael closed his eyes and turned around to let the water hit directly on his back. He then reached behind himself and spread his butt cheeks to let the warmth hit every crevice. As he turned his head and opened his eyes to locate a bar of soap, he didn't see one in the dish under his shower head, so he looked across the room. The two guys who were enjoying each other's company were now soaping up with the other three guys. Hands were everywhere. Michael's dick started getting hard, but at this point, he didn't care.

The cook grabbed Michael's arm and placed a bar of soap in his hand.

"Is this what you're looking for?" he asked Michael.

Michael thanked him and started lathering up his hair and then his face. He rinsed the soap from his head, and then he started with his shoulders and worked the lather slowly down his big, pumped, hairy, muscular body. He enjoyed every inch of himself. He slowly soaped his raging nine-by-seven-inch boner and lathered his hairy, buffalo balls. The guys were watching him and from the looks of their own boners were enjoying the show. That didn't stop Michael.

He bent over to soap up his legs, and when he did, he felt a hand on his back. The cook, with his own bar of soap, proceeded to lather up Michael's back, and when Michael stood up, the cook put one hand on Michael's shoulder, and with the other, he lathered Michael's large, round, muscular ass. He was gentle in his touch. The cook squatted down and lathered Michael's legs, slowly with up and down strokes. Michael resumed lathering his chest, stomach, arms, shoulders, and neck. Then, the cook rose and lathered Michael's ass and back again. With his other hand, the cook reached around and put his meaty paw on Michael's aching cock. The huge, mushroom head was swollen, and his balls were ready for release.

Michael continued to lather his chest, shoulders, biceps, triceps, and forearms, and he reached around to lather his own huge lats.

The cook firmly but slowly stroked Michael's hard soapy cock, and after just a few seconds, Michael shuttered and blew a load into the center of the shower room. The sight of Michael coming sent the other five muscle-heads over the edge, and each of them spunked the shower room floor, too. The cook's own large dick creamed Michael's hip, and he continued to stroke Michael's cock until he was sure those big balls were empty.

With everyone's needs fulfilled, the men in the shower finished rinsing themselves off and left the shower room without saying a word, the cook and Michael included.

Michael pulled on his sweats and slipped into his hi-tops, carrying his briefs, tank top and socks back to his room.

He then changed into a fresh pair of white briefs, jeans and an orange T-shirt and walked over to the diner. Michael took a seat at the counter, and the cook came out in the same outfit he was wearing when Michael first met him. Nothing was said of what just took place in the shower.

Michael understood that it was just men, big muscular men, bonding after a good, healthy workout.

The cook smiled at Michael and recommended the fried chicken, mashed potatoes, green beans and cornbread. Michael didn't argue. He trusted the cook's judgment, and with the first bite, he knew the cook was right.

While he was enjoying a cup of coffee and fresh apple pie, the cook came over to Michael and leaned on the counter in front of him.

"So, what's your business in town," the cook asked.

"I am here to meet with the Mayor about some government business," Michael said.

"At ten tomorrow morning?" the cook asked.

Michael looked at him and asked, "Are you the Mayor, too?"

"And your last name must be Greenberg," the cook said.

They both laughed.

"Good," the cook said, "Tomorrow, after our meeting, you can come back over to the gym, and I will put you through a *real* work out."

And Michael asked, "How many push-ups can you do?"

Two years later, Michael bought the house across the street, and he always showered at the gym after his workouts.

THE GUY DOWN THE HALL

I really dreaded moving out to a complex in the burbs, but after my upstairs neighbor shot her husband and missed sending a bullet through her floor and into my apartment, my friends convinced me it was time.

So, here I was in one of those secure buildings with 500 neighbors. That is 500 people who walk by you without smiling, who look at you strangely when you say hello, and who turn up their noses when they see your dog, even though it is a pet-friendly building. I always lived in bad neighborhoods, where people say hello because if you don't know your neighbors, you won't know whether someone is a gang member, mugger or a rapist. It is not that I was too poor to move; I was just too comfortable, paying a low rent and making excuses.

After a few weeks, I made up my mind that no one was going to say hello and that was just how it is with this "station of society" as Hyacinth Bucket would say on *Keeping Up Appearances*. I came back from walking my dog, who was in her twilight years, when the fire alarm went off. I never lived in a building with an alarm, so I scooped up my dog (she had gone deaf and partially blind by then, so in order to evacuate, it was better that I carry her), and we made our way to the stairs. I had moved to the top floor for obvious reasons (bullets tend to go down rather than up). Outside it was raining, and all I was wearing at the time was an undershirt and shorts. After fifteen minutes, we were given the all clear and made our way upstairs. The whole way, no one said a word. They didn't even comment about my dog and why I was carrying her.

Once on our floor, I put Lucille down, and we walked back to my apartment. As we reached my door, my neighbor from around the corner came around and said, "Hey, I see we had another false alarm."

I was surprised for two reasons. One, he said something to me, and two, he was wearing a sleeveless shirt and boxers. What a sight. He was a little over six feet, maybe a drop over two hundred pounds, with dark hair and eyes and the most fit build I had ever seen, or could see from what was exposed. He was also half my age at around twenty-five.

I had picked up Lucille at that point to keep her from running into him, being partially blind and all, and that made my bicep bulge. I should let you know that I am over six feet myself and close to two-hundred-sixty pounds and a professional trainer and competitive bodybuilder. Approaching fifty, when not in competition, I carry an extra inch or two around the waist, and that is all I will admit.

"False alarm?"

"Yeah, the burger joint downstairs tends to set off alarms all the time. My name's Matt, by the way."

"Nice to meet you," I said as I extended my right hand and shook his. I also put Lucille back down on the floor. "This is Lucille; she's pretty old, deaf and partially blind; that's why I picked her up, so she wouldn't bang into you." And then I shut up, realizing I was giving more information than was necessary and probably because this was the first conversation I had with anyone since I moved in.

"And, your name?" he asked.

"Oh, yeah. I'm Martin."

At that point he started staring at my arms, and my shirt was still wet from the rain, so his eyes glanced over my pecs as well. "Hey, my fiancé and I are throwing a little party tomorrow night around seven. Come on over. We're in five-eighteen."

"Sounds good," I answered and watched as he turned and went back to his apartment. I also hoped he never wore more than a T-shirt and boxers in the future.

As it turned out, I answered too quickly, since I already had plans the next night with a couple of friends to have dinner. So, the next afternoon, I bought a bottle of wine and knocked on five-eighteen.

Matt answered the door, dressed similarly to the night before.

"Hey, Martin, what's up?"

I handed him the wine and said, "I answered too quickly. I have plans tonight, and I didn't want to blow you guys off and just not show up. Here, this is a thank you for the invitation."

"You didn't have to do that," he said in protest.

"I insist. My mother raised me right," I answered. "Can I ask you a question?"

"Sure."

"Do you own pants?" I asked with a grin.

He laughed, and I heard a woman's voice in the background, "I'm so glad you said that." She appeared from another room, and was she gorgeous and a little thing about half his size. "I'm Gina. Thank you for the wine. I'm sorry you can't make it. He promised to wear pants tonight."

We laughed, and I said my goodbyes.

It was a few weeks before I saw him again. I go to the gym very early and am usually out the door around a quarter to five in the morning. I ran into him one morning as he was headed to his gym, and we exchanged pleasantries, and this became an occasional occurrence. Although beautiful to behold, I made up my mind after meeting his fiancé that he was off limits, and I was never into "flipping" guys anyway. I am too old to go around blowing straight guys, besides I never saw the thrill in that. I never said it out loud, but anyone can figure out I am a big fag from the rainbow Mezuzah on my door frame to the rainbow Star of David tattoo on my shoulder to the parade of flaming queens, who are my friends, who would drop by for dinner. Besides a fifty-year-old personal trainer/competitive bodybuilder is a dead giveaway.

One morning as I headed out my door to the gym, I saw a shirtless body walk by and noticed it was Matt. He was wearing very short, gray running shorts that were not unlike the ones President Clinton would wear early in his administration. I yelled at his back, "It is freezing outside. I just came back from walking Lucille."

He stopped and turned around, and I saw his bare torso for the first time. He didn't shave and had the perfect amount of dark hair and that theory about him having the most fit body I ever saw was confirmed. I immediately thought that if this guy has a big dick there is *no* God.

"They say it's seventy outside." He smiled that beautiful smile as I said this.

I walked up to him and got a better look and thanked myself for putting on a tight jock that morning. (I said I was not into flipping straight guys, but that didn't mean he couldn't turn me on.)

We walked over to the elevator and stepped in.

He hit the L and asked if I had an early client.

"No, just working out this morning," I answered.

"Cool, we should work out together sometime," he said.

And then, my odd sense of humor took over when I asked, "Can I pull one of your nipples?"

He looked right at me, smiled and said, "I wish you would."

And, I did. And he leaned in and planted his mouth on mine while simultaneously hitting the red button, stopping the elevator between floors. His tongue was down my throat before I could protest, and I decided not to protest and felt up that perfect body.

I finally came up for air and with a gasp asked, "What about your fiancé?"

"We're both bi," he said and proceeded to remove my shirt and pull down my shorts.

In the time it took for me to fully comprehend what he said, my jock was around my ankles, and my dick was in his mouth. He had pulled his shorts down and was stroking his cock while working mine, and I figured we didn't have a lot of time, and he figured we didn't have a lot of time, and he sucked me for points and knew I would blow any minute, and I tried to get him off my dick, so I could get at his, but he was insistent, and I just shot my load, and he swallowed every drop while jerking his and shooting between my legs and hitting the wall of the elevator. It all happened so fast, that I was still comprehending what happened when he stood up, pulled up his shorts, and I retrieved my shirt, jock and shorts, and he hit the button, and we stepped out of the elevator.

"Have a good run," I said as he took off.

A few weeks later, his fiancé went to visit her parents, and he came over, and we did it again. This time, however, we took our time. He has since married Gina, and their wedding was beautiful. And on occasion, he stops by for a little pre-run work out.

CLOTHING OPTIONAL

After a seven-hour drive through rural southwestern Virginia, a few miles across the Tennessee line, and down a very dusty country road, I arrived at the TimberBear Campground. I had read about it online and decided to try a different kind of vacation, but after being buzzed through the gate, if you want to call it a gate, and driving up to the main cabin, if you want to call it a cabin, I was beginning to rethink my idea of an alternative getaway.

Between the geezer who checked me in and the one who pointed out my cabin, there were a total of seven teeth. I drove down the hill to the far side of the grounds past what I assumed was the pool and bath house, a couple of campers and trailers, and spotted little duplex-like cabins lined up in a row. Mine was number 6–6B to be exact since it was a duplex of sorts.

It may have been late September, but the weather begged to differ, with temperatures in the nineties and not a cloud in sight. I heard they were suffering through a drought, and by the looks of the layer of dust on my 1975 AMC Matador Coupe, they weren't kidding.

What I didn't see were very many people. I guessed it was late in the season, which was fine, since I am not fond of crowds. I parked around back and unpacked my car. Being this was a clothing optional campground, I didn't have to pack a hundred outfits for a change the way I did for that miserable cruise my best friend talked me into taking.

"Nice ride," came a voice from behind me.

"Thanks."

"1974?"

I turned to face what appeared to be a post-op FTM transsexual wearing only cut-off shorts. "1975 AMC Matador Coupe Barcelona Edition ... it was my grandmother's."

He walked over to my car, and I hastily walked around front to 6B, opened the door and took in the décor. 'Early trailer park' would best describe the room, for the cabin was just that, a room. There was a bathroom with a shower stall, and that was about it.

I unpacked what few things I had with me then changed into my swim trunks to take in what little daylight was left in the afternoon. I don't know why I put on my swim trunks since they would be coming off as soon as I arrived at the pool.

I am a former powerlifter and have continued to work out hard since ending my competition days in the late 80s, which enables me to maintain my thickly muscled physique. I am not what you would call bodybuilder cut, but at five-eleven and over 270 pounds, I am a lot of man, and I have a pretty thick cock and big balls that swing nicely if I do say so myself. I am not self- conscious about my body, but I am aware that there are those with a lot more 'definition' and much prettier faces. The best way to describe my face is that it is that of a bouncer, which is what I do for a living, and my nose has taken its share of punishment as well as my jaw. I get my share of ass when I want it, but I have found that as I grow older and especially after 'a certain age,' I don't crave it as much as I used to. I figure I have done all I care to do in bed, so if I find myself rolling around naked with someone, it better be special.

I chose an empty chaise at the pool, which wasn't difficult since there were about four people there, and took off my trunks, lay down and took in what sun was left for the day.

I was bored already.

After what seemed hours, but was only about thirty minutes, I gathered my things and made my way back to my cabin.

I was kind of tired from the drive and having put in a long shift the night before, so I took a shower in the tiny stall and decided to take a nap.

I never realize how tired I was. When I opened my eyes, it was pitch black in the cabin, and the clock next to the bed indicated it was 2:11 – AM! I hadn't slept like that in years. I was sprawled out naked on top of the bed and sporting an erection that could hammer nails.

I got out of bed and looked out the window. There was no one around or lights on, so I opened the door and stepped outside, stark naked and still pretty hard. I stretched my arms and let out a big yawn, when I heard, "Hello." I just about jumped out of my skin.

I had a neighbor in my duplex. Standing at just over six feet, he wasn't a bad looking one either. He was around my age, bald, with a mustache, a nice muscular hairy chest – and everything else – and wearing boxer briefs. I immediately hid my cock with my hand.

"Hey, sorry about that ... I didn't think anyone would be out here."

"No problem," he replied then he turned his attention back to his cell phone. "I can't get any bars."

"Isn't it late to be making calls?" I asked while still standing there willing my dick to go down, which it eventually did.

"I've been trying to get a hold of our office overseas all day. Ahh fuck it," he said, then flipped his phone shut. "I guess I should just go to sleep."

"I just woke up from a nine-hour nap," I said with a laugh. "I think I'll see if the pool is open all night."

"The pool is closed, but the steam room and sauna are open all night. They're in the bath house right next to it," he said, obviously having visited here before.

"Thanks, either one sounds good right now."

He went back into his cabin, and I into mine. I brushed my teeth to get rid of the dead rat taste and hoped my breath didn't offend my neighbor. I grabbed two towels – one to sit on in the sauna or steam room and one to dry off with. I didn't bother putting on a pair of shorts and just wrapped a towel around my waist, and slipped on my flip-flops, grabbed a jug of water, then stepped out.

The steam room looked as if a sloppy orgy was played out just hours before, so I chose the sauna. After figuring out how to switch it on, filling the bucket with water to pour over the coals, I hung one towel on a hook outside the door, and slipped off the towel around my waist and laid it on the bench, sat down, leaned back, closed my eyes and relaxed.

I started to sweat almost immediately and took a healthy swig from the jug of water. I then wiped the sweat from my chest down my stomach and along my cock, which started getting hard again. I didn't care, figuring no one was going to come in at this hour, and if they did, whatever.

Wiping sweat across my cock turned into gentle stroking until it was standing right up again ready to do some carpentry work. I closed my eyes and continued gently stroking my dick.

I was starting to feel pretty relaxed and a bit horny when the door to the sauna opened. I opened my eyes and saw that my cabin mate had entered, and this time he wasn't wearing the boxer briefs.

He walked right over to me without saying a word, leaned down and planted his mouth on mine. We proceeded to make out and wrestle our tongues, while he reached down and grabbed my dick, and I switched my hand from my dick to his, which was also ready to hammer a few nails and had the heft to do so.

The guy was a great kisser, and he apparently thought I was to, which I am of course, but his moans didn't hurt my ego. When his mouth left mine, I missed it immediately, until he hopped up on the bench with his feet on either side of me, his hands on the wall behind me, and his huge cock pointed at my face.

I opened my mouth, let him shove it in, and grabbed his balls. He fucked my throat like a champ, and I didn't gag at all. When I could feel he was getting close, he increased his rhythm, then pulled out and shot a big load all over my face while I held onto his balls.

When he was drained, he hopped down from the bench, got down on his knees and swallowed my cock. It only took a few seconds for him to empty my balls into his hungry mouth. He then stood up, leaned in and licked my face clean before planting his mouth on mine again as we tasted our comingled loads in his mouth.

He then winked, turned around and left.

I never saw him again.

A MARRIED MAN

I should know better. He's married with kids. He has one car he shares with his wife. He can only stop by for twenty minutes and with only ten minutes notice.

I get a text. "What's up?"

I answer, "My cock."

Same crap every time. He isn't even that good-looking. I mean, he works out and all, but his body is nothing worth writing home to Mom about. If I did write home to Mom, the only thing I could say is he's Jewish. "Oh, and by the way, he's married, too, and on the down-low."

Good thing my mother is dead. This would kill her for sure. I can hear her now. "What? There are no nice Jewish unmarried boys? You have to go after a closet case?"

Strangely, I met him on a sex line. Or maybe not so strangely. Where else would he go for sex? Synagogue? Please.

I remember that first meeting. No head shot, just a body shot. I remember seeing his face for the first time. Ugly is the best way to describe it. He was bald with a big nose and squinty eyes. I let him in anyway. I guess I am just a pig for sex. I could do better, not a lot better, but certainly better than this troll. His dick wasn't that big, but the cock-ring didn't hurt.

I wondered when he put that on. Did his wife see him in it?

However, the sex was pretty good. It wasn't the best, but it was worth a repeat. But, a repeat was next to impossible.

I'd text him, and he'd say he couldn't get away. Or worse, he was headed to a "buddy's" house for a three-way. He thought it was cool to tell me that. The man was a bigger slut than I – and an asshole to boot.

So, why do I continue to stay in touch? I actually erased his number from my phone, only to have him text me for a hook-up out of the blue. And, twice he would contact me, get me all horned up, only to cancel at the last minute because he was dealing with his daughter's teenage drama of some sort.

Yet, here I sit.

It's Sunday afternoon. I should go to the gym, take a nap, read a book, do something constructive. But, he texted me. Now, I am hard as a rock. I don't know why. As I said, he's ugly, he's married, and more importantly, he's selfish.

There is no future with this guy. He isn't going to leave his wife. And, he certainly isn't going to leave her for me. I know that. I am not as dumb as I look.

We have already texted at least ten times. Now, he is having trouble finding an excuse to leave the house with their only car. He asks me for an excuse. What the fuck do I know? I am not married, and I haven't been in the closet since kindergarten. If I want to get laid, I just get in my car and go.

Four hours have gone by, and I have wasted an entire afternoon. It is near dinner time. I have to work tomorrow. I am past my need for dick now. I keep giving him fifteen more minutes before I start making dinner and forget about the whole thing.

I receive one final text. "Sorry, stud. It ain't gonna work tonight."

I don't even answer. I erase his number. I am done ...

... at least until the next time he sends me a text.

CONFERENCE CALL

I had been camming with Jeff for years. We met on Bigmuscle then exchanged Yahoo IDs and would cam and flex every couple of months. He was in the business like me, so I knew he would be discreet. Besides, if he sold a video of me, I could do the same to him.

He lived 3,000 miles away. I felt as if I knew him intimately. We would strip then flex, then jerk off for each other. We told each other our fantasies. He would tell me how he wanted to sit in my lap while I flexed and fucked him; I told him he needed to sit on my face first. It was harmless camming, so I told him things I wanted to do that were not usually part of my routine. But, it was all in good fun.

I bought a new computer with a cam built in, so I wanted to try it out. Well, the cam was on the top of the screen, so I had to fold it a bit to get a good shot, but that limited my ability to see what he was doing, so I bought an external cam to enjoy as well as put on a show.

I am usually pretty good with computers, so hooking up the external cam was easy enough.

I was on a video conference call with my agent and manager, when my Yahoo IM popped up with a message from Jeff. I told him to give me about thirty minutes until I finished up this call.

A half hour later, I ended the call with my guys, and sent an IM to Jeff that I could 'play' now.

And, as usual, we were naked in seconds, flexing and showing off.

I had slipped on a cock ring and was greasing up my dick, while he did the same. In between, I would wipe off my hands and type up some nasty message; he would then reply with something even nastier.

Occasionally, I would tease him by rubbing my thumb on the head of my dick, then trailing a string of precum up to my mouth and licking my thumb clean. He loved that, being as much of a cum pig as I was.

His favorite thing was for me to flex my bicep right up to the camera, and when he was ready to come, he would beg me to do that. I liked watching him flex his legs and muscular butt.

We were really going at it today, and I was standing, naked, flexing, all oiled up and stroking away. I was getting close, so I gave him a thumbs up. I then let go of my dick, flexed both biceps and came without touching myself. My dick shot up high and quite a few times, then a few extra spurts dripped down the length of my dick and onto my balls while I continued to flex.

He came, too, all over his hairy belly.

I waved goodbye; he did the same. Then, I cleaned myself up before turning off the cam.

My Skype buzzed. It was my agent.

I clicked him on after slipping on a T-shirt.

"I just figured out how to jump start your career," he said.

I didn't realize both web cams were going at once. Since the one he was watching was the one that was part of the computer with the bad angle I mentioned earlier, all he got was the neck down.

The video went viral in about an hour. The interviews requests poured in, and I neither denied nor admitted that it was my body.

I just signed a four picture deal with a major studio.

I specified no nude scenes in my contract.

Oh, and Jeff? He is directing one of the pictures. We finally are going to meet face-to-face.

THE LAB RAT

Dr. Musclestein had a theory. Anyone could achieve the results of a steroid user, provided they had proper nutrition, access to the best weight training equipment available, unlimited time, and encouragement.

He had a state-of-the-art gym built in a wing of his home, complete with kitchenette, bedroom, full bath, and French doors leading to his backyard swimming pool. The subject of his experiment would be required to live in that wing of the house for thirty days. His waking hours would mostly be spent working out. He would also be eating quality proteins, fresh fruits and vegetables, and he would have daily, two-hour tanning privileges by the pool. However, no television would be allowed. When he was not eating or sleeping, he was to be working out. His muscles would be pumped during all his waking hours, forcing them to grow beyond anyone's expectations.

However, to test his theory, Dr. Musclestein needed a lab rat. He searched high and low across the local college campus, but there were no candidates who fit the bill. He visited all the local gyms, but no one was right for the job. He even scoured the beaches. There were those who were willing to be his subjects, but all had been on the 'juice.'

He needed a natural bodybuilder, and he was disappointed. All this expense to build the perfect lab, and he could not carry out his experiment. He was about to give up, when he noticed the man mowing his lawn. This was not his usual gardener. Bobby, his gardener, was in his sixties and although in good shape for his age, he was no muscle man. But Bobby's replacement was exactly what the Doctor had ordered.

Dr. Musclestein had an idea, but he would need to get dressed first. He usually walked around his home in nothing but black sweat pants. To look at him, one would have thought he had already tried out his theory on himself. He was six-foot-five and 260 pounds of smooth, rock-hard muscle. Everything about him rippled and bulged. But, if he was going to approach the gardener about his experiment, he needed to dress the part. He changed into gray slacks, a white shirt, striped tie, a lab coat and his black framed bifocals.

As he stepped out the back door, he spotted the gardener, who just at that moment was taking off his shirt. The man was five-foot-nine and looked to weigh around 190 pounds. He was hairy and thickly muscled. Dr. Musclestein guessed him to be Italian, and when the thirty-four-year-old man introduced himself as Scott Manicotti, his heritage was confirmed. Scott wore his black hair in a crew cut and also had a goatee. The doctor thought to himself, *If this guy is not gay, he missed an excellent opportunity.*

Dr. Musclestein explained his theory to Scott, who seemed more interested than any of the other potential subjects, and that afternoon, Scott moved into the lab wing of the house. Dr. Musclestein kept the door to the lab locked in the event that Scott might try to escape, which would cause him to have to start his experiment anew. However, since Scott had been there, he did not complain once. He enjoyed being able to work out all hours of the day and night.

Every day, Dr. Musclestein would unlock the door and enter the lab with two bags of fresh groceries – the highest quality proteins, fresh fruits and vegetables, and plenty of bottled water. After putting the groceries away, he would observe his lab rat, who could always be found working out. The lab rat, as per the doctor's instructions, wore minimal clothing, preferring only a jock strap, sweat socks and sneakers.

Dr. Musclestein would pull out his tape measure and chart the lab rat's progress. He would carefully measure his biceps, pecs, waist, glutes, thighs, and calves. The lab rat was doing well and had already put on ten pounds of solid muscle. His thick build had evolved into a ripped display of hairy, masculine strength.

Dr. Musclestein was pleased with the results, and every day, he would take the prior day's dirty jock straps and sweat socks and lock the door. After returning to his section of the home, he would strip off his lab coat, shirt, tie and slacks and stroke his thick, hard cock, while sniffing the lab rat's dirty jock, until he covered his smooth chest and belly in cum.

During the third week, Dr. Musclestein was so pleased with the lab rat's progress, he decided to give him a treat. He usually did not check in on his subject any time after the morning progress report, but he decided to surprise the lab rat this particular afternoon.

He unlocked the door, and he was surprised not to find his subject working out. However, he did hear the shower going. Dr. Musclestein placed the tray he was carrying on the kitchenette counter and sat down on one of the stools, waiting for the lab rat to finish scrubbing up.

He heard the squeaking sound of faucets being turned off and the shower door being opened. A few seconds later, the lab rat appeared. He was stark naked, pumped as usual and dripping wet. Dr. Musclestein was pleased with his progress scoping out the subject's beautiful muscles, especially the thick one that was hanging between his legs. The lab rat saw the tray and asked about it.

Dr. Musclestein pointed to the cake and ice cream on the tray and said, "I think you have worked very hard, and I brought you a reward." He then motioned for the lab rat to sit on the stool facing him and not bother putting on any clothes.

The Doctor looked him over admiring the results of his experiment. He then grabbed a spoon and proceeded to feed the lab rat. The more he fed him, the more he fell in love with him. The lab rat looked up at the doctor and opened his mouth invitingly with each spoonful of cake and ice cream.

The doctor scooted in closer and placed a hand on the lab rat's thigh while continuing to feed him his treat, spoonful by loving spoonful. His hand slid up the lab rat's thigh until he reached the prize. As he stroked the subject's hardening cock, he continued to spoon feed him. Precum was leaking heavily from the lab rat's dick, and he used the goo to slick it up and increase his stroke.

And, they never took their eyes off each other.

The doctor put down the spoon and leaned in, gently kissing his subject, tasting the cake and ice cream and exploring the lab rat's mouth with his tongue. His cock started to pulse as their lips moved across each other and their tongues intertwined.

Dr. Musclestein got up from the stool and leaned down in front of his subject. He removed his hand from the throbbing dick and with his mouth tasted a steady stream of sweet and salty precum, and as he cupped the large hairy balls that hung from the lab rat, he heard a quickening of breath, and felt the first shots of many of the subject's sweet, thick load hitting the back of his throat. He did not take his mouth off the cock until he knew it was completely drained.

Dr. Musclestein got up and sat back down on the stool, and the two of them kissed, tasting the load that was just released. They kissed for a long time, acknowledging their love for each other.

When they released their lips, the lab rat looked deeply into the eyes of the doctor.

"That was hot, really hot," Scott said.

"I couldn't help myself; you look incredible," Dr. Musclestein said. "Apparently, my theory works."

Scott looked down at himself, pleased with his progress. The doctor ran the back of his hand across the young man's hairy body.

"You know I have to be back to work tomorrow," Scott said.

"Yeah," the doctor acknowledged.

Scott stood up and put on a fresh jock. He looked over at the doctor and said, "Next month, I get to be Dr. Musclestein, OK?"

"Anything for you, baby," Dr. Musclestein answered and smiled as he realized how lucky he was that they still enjoyed these games eight years after they first met.

BITCH, PLEASE

I had pretty much given up on dating. It was always the same thing. The guy would come on strong the week before the date, being all charming and sexy. Then, we would go on the date, have a pretty good time, maybe even have a second date. After that, we would make plans for another date. A few days later, I would get the message that he wasn't feeling well. Then, he would have the flu. Then, he would cancel. And of course, we would never see each other again.

Sure I had been on dates, when I didn't want to see the guy again, but I have balls, and I would be honest up front and say that I either didn't see a future in this, or this wouldn't work out, or I just wasn't interested in him.

I don't play games. I don't tease. I don't bullshit around. Maybe this is why I am single. I just don't put up with guys' crap.

Am I that repulsive? No. As a matter of fact I have been told I am sexy, beautiful, funny, smart, easygoing, you name it.

For the record, I don't consider myself sexy or beautiful. I never go for guys who look like me. I always laugh at those clone couples. It is obvious they find themselves so attractive that every guy they date looks like their twin. If I saw me on the street, I wouldn't give myself a second look.

Do I think I am ugly? Hell no. If I were ugly, would I be America's heartthrob? Would I be openly gay and still be landing roles as a sexy straight man, bedding every young, firm actress in Hollywood?

Women eat me up. Once they see the first fifteen minutes of one of my latest movies, they forget I suck cock and take it up the ass. They believe I am totally into eating pussy and slamming my man-hammer in after I have warmed it up with my sexy mouth.

But, some heartthrob. I cannot get past date number three. Is it the guys I date? Probably. Let's face it. I can't just walk into a club and pick up some guy anonymously. The paparazzi follow me everywhere.

A lot of guys want my life. Let me tell you. Getting laid when you are famous is not easy. You can't pick up guys online because you don't know what kind of stalker or weirdo you will let into your home. Or, he could go running to the tabloids with all the details.

As I said, I am out, but even if I were straight, I would run into the same issues with some hot chick, who just wanted to sell her story to *The Enquirer*, telling them how big my dick was or how fast I came.

So, how does someone like me get a date? Well, I could date other actors, but I find them so self-absorbed, and they can be worse than those outside the business. Most are closeted, and the others are just looking for a way to advance their careers. Therefore, I depend on friends or those I meet through my charity work.

Hard to believe that someone as famous as I does charity work, isn't it? Well, my uncle always said you have to give something back. I feel very fortunate to have the life I have, and when I am on a break from filming, I devote my time to those who need it most – animals. I enjoy this part of my life more than the work some times.

I may come across as a hard ass or a heartless bitch, but one has to be tough to have made it as long as I have in this business. I have been acting since I was nine years old, so I don't know any other world. But, I know that if I never became an actor, I would have had a career where I helped animals.

I met Tyler at an adopt-a-pet given by a local animal rescue organization. He was also a volunteer. The first thing I noticed was how the volunteer T-shirt hugged his body. The second thing I noticed was that he was more about doing the dirty work than telling me how much he loved my movies and crap. The third thing was his sense of humor. He made me laugh. This is a huge plus in my book. Usually, I am the one who has to be entertaining.

We spent the day talking to people as they came by to see the dogs. He and I also walked the dogs around the venue, so they wouldn't get keyed up from sitting for so long. And, we chatted and joked around the whole time.

I found out he was a director of public relations for a local charity and had only lived in Los Angeles for a couple of months. He didn't like bars or crowds, and the only hobby he had was the gym.

At the end of the day, I did something I never did. I gave him my private number. Usually, if I was to set up a date, I would have my assistant field the calls in case I was murdered. That way they could find the killer through his cell-phone records.

We texted and talked for two weeks. He was going back east for a wedding the weekend between, so we set our first date for the weekend after. I was excited about going out with Tyler. He seemed different from all the others. We had the same passions and the same warped sense of humor.

The Saturday of our date came, and he was running late, so he called because his GPS could not find my street. I knew it wouldn't and told him so. My street is fairly new and unless you've updated your system in the last month or so, you won't find it.

I talked him to my home. I didn't ask him what he was driving. I guessed it would be a black BMW. It was. When I saw it approach the gate on my security camera, I buzzed him in.

We decided to go out to dinner. There is a nice Italian restaurant not far from where I live that is way off the beaten path, and no one has ever bothered me there. I let him drive, since a black car would be unnoticeable in LA. Who doesn't have a black BMW in this town? Oh yeah, I don't.

Dinner was nice, and he ate like a horse, which is another turn on. I get so sick of guys who won't touch a piece of bread or salad dressing or dessert.

We came back to my place, and I took my dogs for a walk. He came with us. I already knew he liked dogs, and he was kind to the waiter in the restaurant.

You know what they say. Watch how a man treats dogs and waiters and that is how he will treat you.

I suggested watching a little television. Being in the business, there are two things I hardly have time to do – go to movies or watch TV. Can you believe it? I am usually on a set for twelve to fifteen hours a day, so who has the time?

We happened upon this show called *Drop Dead Diva*. I had heard about it, and there was some kind of marathon of first-season episodes on Lifetime, 'television for women and gay men.' We settled in. I fell in love with the show, and so did he. I had to get a box of Kleenex after the first couple of hours because we were crying at the sentimentality of it.

I made a mental note to call my agent and ask him to get me a guest spot on the show. I also found the actress who played the fat girl to be the most attractive woman I had seen in a long time. I like big women, and Brooke Elliot is just breathtaking. Tyler agreed.

After episode five, we started making out. He was probably the best kisser I had ever had the pleasure of tonguing. I was hard in an instant. This went on for a good hour before I led him to my bedroom.

That is when things got really hot and heavy. I slowly removed his shirt to reveal a very hairy, muscular body. I was so glad he didn't shave his chest. I ran my face along his torso and bit his nipples, which apparently, he loved. It took a while to unbutton his jeans, and he managed to get mine off a lot quicker. We continued making out, biting, licking, and feeling with our briefs on. Mine were black with white stripes; his were red with black stripes. Both pairs were wet with precum stains.

Finally naked, we really got down to business. I don't know who was more into oral, but we competed with who could suck the best and longest. I think he won. I then flipped him on his stomach and took a dive for his hairy ass, but not before I admired his muscular legs. I never saw such muscular legs in my life. He flexed them for me, and I was his forever.

His ass was a true delight. I kidded him about how it glowed in the dark, being so white against his tan skin. Mine is the same shade as the rest of me because I suntan nude on my private pool deck.

I ate him out as if they had not served me enough at dinner. My tongue gave his pucker a good workout, then I worked a wet finger into his hole, and he moaned and wiggled his butt.

He begged me to fuck him. So, I put on a raincoat, lubed up my pole and his hole, and I slowly entered him while he moaned and pushed back wanting more and more of my dick.

Tyler was so sensual and so sexy and so nice and so funny and so my type, that I decided to forego the usual Olympic-style fucking I usually perform and give him a slow, easy, loving fuck.

I reached around and pinched his nipples while I licked his neck and fucked him all the way in, and all the way out. He was moaning and begging for more and telling me how much he loved it. I was able to keep up for some time, and after a long while, he announced he was going to come.

He came all over the sheets underneath us, and the feeling of his pulsing ass made me come as well, filling the condom completely.

I asked him to spend the night. But, he said it was best he went home. However, he asked if we could get together the next night. I, of course, said yes.

I slept well that night. In the morning, I knew I would get the usual text message. You know the one. It is the one you get after a long while of hot and heavy communications followed by a phenomenal date and earth moving sex.

My phone buzzed around ten in the morning. There was a text message.

"I woke up feeling like hell. I won't be able to make it tonight. How about next weekend?"

I just rolled my eyes. I texted back, "Wow. Guys usually wait until the second or third date to get sick, and then we never see each other again. Feel better."

It is amazing how predictable some people are. I called that one the minute he begged me to fuck him. Some call this psychic ability.

I call it "bitch, please."

A JEW FOR ALL SEASONS

For Sammy, Christmas was his least favorite time of year. The season always annoyed him, for he felt bombarded by reindeer, snowmen, Santas, elves, stockings and everything else that made the season unbearable. He remembered the other kids teasing him about being Jewish when he was growing up in the South, but what he hated most was being asked, "Is Hanukah the Jewish Christmas?" He would always answer, "No. Christmas is the Jewish Christmas. Jesus was Jewish, Mary and Joseph were Jewish, and at least one of the Wise Men was Jewish. That would be the one who brought the fur." He would then go on to tell them that Christmas was not Jesus's birthday as he was born during the month of *Elul*, which falls in August or September, depending on the lunar calendar cycle. But, they weren't interested in education, and he would be beaten up by a gang of them during this time of peace and holiness, for ridiculing their yuletide cheer.

So, it was ironic that during the recession of 2008, Sammy, would find himself grateful to have a job as a department store Santa, for he had been almost nine months without full-time employment. He was also grateful for Christmas Eve as that marked his last day in the red fat suit. December 24 also marked the last day he would have to work with Marvin, the ornery elf they assigned to him for the prior month. To make the day even more special, the last kid to sit on Sammy's lap lacked bladder control.

Both Sammy and Marvin had similar features, dark curly hair cut short, piercing green eyes, olive-toned skin and full lips, but that was where the similarities ended. Sammy was over six-foot-two, and Marvin was a little over four feet.

Sammy walked back to the dressing room that was reserved for Santa and his helpers to change and quickly stripped himself of his costume. He no sooner had put on his jeans and sweatshirt when Marvin walked in and began to strip.

"Fucking brats," the holiday elf said as he took off his green felt shirt.

Sammy didn't bother to look at the little guy because his attitude was a turn off, nor did he respond.

"I'll bet you're glad this gig is over," Marvin continued.

"Yeah, but I do hate to lose the paycheck," Sammy answered.

"Me, too. It's been tough finding a job."

Sammy wanted to comment on Marvin's attitude being a hindrance to finding gainful employment, but he just was not in the mood to get into a conversation with him, and now that this job was over, he didn't have to.

"You want to get a drink?" Marvin asked.

Sammy, who had his backpack over one shoulder and was heading out of the dressing room, turned around and gave Marvin a look of disbelief.

"Well?"

"It's just that you've been pretty much an asshole this past month, and you haven't said two words directly to me since we started. Now you want to go out for a drink?" Sammy asked.

"Yeah. Look, I hated this gig, and besides you tall people always get to play Santa while the real elves," and Marvin gestured to himself as if on display, "don't get to play the jolly ole St. Nick. So, forgive me if I'm not such a happy leprechaun. I also don't care too much for the goyim or their spoiled kids."

"You're Jewish?" Sammy asked.

"My name is Marvin Minkoff."

"Who knew? Mine is Sammy Sagman," he said with a smile.

"I know. I looked at your application after they hired you. What do you know? Two members of the tribe celebrating *their* lord and savior's birth," Marvin said as he put on his jacket.

"Which took place during *Elul*," Sammy said. "What the hell? Let's go get a drink."

Marvin grabbed his backpack, and they headed out of the department store and down the street looking for a bar that might be open. Sammy knew of a leather bar around the corner, but he wasn't sure if Marvin swung that way. They walked a couple of blocks before Marvin stopped.

"There's the Falcon, Down Under's, the Garage ... pick one," Marvin said.

Realizing Marvin did swing that way, Sammy picked the Garage as it was the only one quiet enough to allow for a conversation. Sammy suggested they put their backpacks in the trunk of his car, so they doubled back to the parking lot, ditched their backpacks, and walked the four blocks to the Garage.

As it turned out, Marvin was not the jerk Sammy thought he was; he just wasn't happy about his employment situation, and being a little person made it that much harder to find a job as many potential employers did not take him seriously when he came in for an interview. Sammy couldn't quite figure out what Marvin did for a living, but it sounded a bit like an assembly-line supervisor or a social worker. And, Sammy didn't bother interrogating him too much. Sammy was a print production manager before the company where he worked went under.

Around eleven, they decided to call it a night. They walked back to Sammy's car to retrieve Marvin's backpack before Sammy drove home.

"Do you need a ride?" Sammy asked as he closed the trunk.

"That's OK; I can catch the bus."

"Don't be ridiculous, besides, it's Christmas Eve; where are you going to get a bus at this hour?" Sammy asked.

"It's just that ..."

"Get in the car," Sammy insisted.

Marvin climbed in, and Sammy asked where he lived. Marvin only gave him cross streets.

When they arrived at the destination, Sammy saw a rundown motel offering weekly rates and efficiencies. He was heartsick. In the few hours he had spent with Marvin, he had grown a little fond of him, and he didn't like the idea of his having to live like this in what was essentially a crack house offering weekly rates.

"Is that where you live?" Sammy asked pointing to the motel across the street.

"Yeah, and don't give me any lectures. I had a nice time tonight and thanks for the ride ..."

"Not so fast," Sammy interrupted. "Go in and get your things. I have a two bedroom apartment. My roommate moved out a while ago, and I need help with the rent. No arguments, you can stay for as little or as long as you want," Sammy said, and he was surprised at how quickly he offered Marvin a place to stay. This was so not like him to let just anyone into his home; however, Sammy was a compassionate person, and he knew he would not be able to sleep nights knowing Marvin was living in these conditions.

"Look, I don't need looking after ..."

"I know, but I am not leaving you here. I don't care how long you've lived here. This isn't safe, and I'm not leaving until we get your things and you come with me. End of discussion," Sammy said as he pulled up to the front of the motel. "What room is yours?"

Marvin stared at him for a second then resigned himself to the fact that he was not going to win this one. "Eight-H."

They gathered Marvin's things, which didn't take long as he pretty much sold everything he owned before moving into this dump. After packing them up in the trunk, Sammy drove them to his apartment. While he did not live in luxury or even the best neighborhood, Sammy's place was a far cry from where Marvin called home.

They carried Marvin's few boxes upstairs, and Sammy directed him to the spare room, which had a dresser, a bed and a nightstand with a lamp. The place was not that large, and they would have to share a bathroom, but Marvin did not complain. He unpacked his things while Sammy puttered around his bedroom getting ready for bed. He took off his shirt as it was unseasonably warm for this time of year and exchanged his jeans for some sweatpants, sans underwear.

He went in to check on Marvin, who had settled in very quickly having put away almost all of his stuff.

"Don't be shy. Help yourself to anything you want in the fridge, and ..." Sammy stopped talking when he noticed Marvin was looking away and apparently had been crying. "Marvin, what's wrong?" Sammy asked as he sat next to Marvin on the bed and put his arm around him.

Marvin wiped his eyes then looked up at Sammy, "I'm sorry. It has just been so hard these last few months, and I was a total dick to you while we were playing Santa and the elf, and here you go and open your home to me ... I ...."

"Please, it's my pleasure. I'm sure you would have done the same for me," Sammy said as he rubbed Marvin's back. "Now, don't say anymore about it. I'm going to take a shower and go to bed. I suggest you do the same. Tomorrow, if anything is open, we'll go and get some groceries and maybe go out for Chinese food." Sammy stood up and winked, and Marvin smiled back. Marvin also took in Sammy's form. Little did anyone realize that under the red fat suit was a hunk of a man, tight with muscle. He also noted how the sweats hugged his round butt as he walked away. Within minutes, Marvin heard the shower running.

Once Sammy was done and out of the bathroom, he called to Marvin to let him know that if he needed a shower, the bathroom was free.

Marvin stripped down and went into the bathroom and turned on the water. Sammy, wearing only a pair of white briefs, reappeared and startled him.

"I'm sorry, I just realized you may not be able to reach the shower head to adjust it," Sammy said as he looked over Marvin, who although a little person around four-feet tall, had an incredible body.

"That would help," Marvin said, "could you just detach the handheld, and I can take it from there."

Sammy detached the handheld shower and let it hang down and stared at Marvin again.

"Excuse me for staring, but you are really built ... I didn't realize ... I mean ..." he stammered.

"That midgets work out?" Marvin said with a chuckle as he stepped into the shower and closed the curtain.

"Yeah," Sammy said as he stayed put while Marvin bathed himself.

"There's a lot you don't know, and besides, a guy has to work out to make it in our world, or he'll never get laid," Marvin said with a laugh.

"I guess there is a lot I need to learn," Sammy said as he exited the bathroom.

After a few minutes, he heard Marvin turn off the shower, and he realized he forgot to put out a towel for him. Sammy immediately jumped out of bed and called out, "I forgot to give you a towel." He grabbed one from the linen closet, and he entered the bathroom right as Marvin opened the shower curtain.

Sammy handed him the towel and looked over Marvin's clean wet body. As his eyes scanned down, he noticed something else about Marvin. He may have been a little person, but that was all that was little about him. He was sporting a beautiful hard-on that was at least eight inches long, maybe longer, and very thick with a mushroom head.

"Sorry, guy, I've been kind of horny lately. I would have polished it off in the shower, but I didn't want to use up all your hot water."

Sammy didn't say a word. He just dropped to his knees and took that big dick into his mouth and started sucking as if he were starving for air and Marvin's tool provided oxygen. Marvin didn't stop him; he just moaned and placed his hands on Sammy's head.

Sammy reached back and removed his underwear to free up his own hard cock, which was an inch shy of Marvin's and not quite as thick. Once naked, he grabbed Marvin's full balls with one hand and felt up and down his compact, muscular body with the other. The whole time, Marvin was still standing in the tub. Sammy didn't care. His cock was heaven, and his precum tasted sweet, very sweet, and there was plenty of it. Sammy couldn't get enough of his cock or the precum he was being fed, and Marvin was not about to stop him. Sammy felt Marvin's balls tighten up and his cock swell even more, and he knew it wouldn't be long. His own cock was throbbing and bobbing and leaking.

"I'm gonna come down your throat if you don't stop," Marvin declared. Sammy just kept at it, sucking that big thick leaking cock as if his life depended on it, and the more he sucked, the more turned on he was. "Here it comes, buddy!"

The first blast went straight back, and more and more cum filled Sammy's mouth, and he didn't lose a drop of the sweet cream. In fact, it was the sweetest load he ever tasted. He just kept sucking and sucking to be sure he didn't miss a drop, and tasting that sweet load brought him over the edge with a hands-free orgasm that blasted the side of the tub. Sucking on Marvin's dick was the greatest sexual experience he had ever had – so far.

When they were spent, Sammy lay down on the floor on his back, his dick still semi-hard, and Marvin stepped out of the tub. Sammy licked his lips.

"Damn, your cum tastes just like ... like ... peppermint!" Sammy said with surprise.

Marvin didn't say a word, leaned over and kissed Sammy while he straddled his chest. The kiss was long, sloppy and deep, just the way Sammy liked it.

They broke away from each other, and Marvin had a glow about him as if he were being bathed in pink lights.

"You have been a good boy this year, Sammy," Marvin said.

Sammy thought he may have had too much to drink at the Garage, for Marvin was transforming. While his hot body and huge dick remained the same, his dark hair grew to his shoulders, and he grew a well-groomed beard.

Sammy was frightened at first until Marvin put a reassuring hand on his chest, which emanated a warmth he never felt before. They were still naked, Sammy on his back on the bathroom floor, and Marvin straddling him. The little man then sat on Sammy's chest, his cock resting on his sternum and pointing at his neck. His velvety balls felt so good against Sammy's skin, they made him tingle with joy.

"Who are you?" Sammy asked.

"My last name is not Minkoff, although I am Jewish," the now long-haired elf said. "I am Santa Claus's twin brother, Marvin Claus. Yeah, I know Claus doesn't sound Jewish, but our name used to be Clausenoffenberg before we changed it. The kids used to have so much trouble with Clausenoffenberg."

"But, Santa is a symbol of Christmas ... I mean Santa does not exist ... I mean ... Oh my God ... does this mean I have to convert?"

"Sammy, my son. The Christians high-jacked us a long, long time ago. We are just part of the Diaspora, who happen to be living at the North Pole. My brother and I are angels. We operate a factory and make toys, but we don't fly around with reindeer and jump down chimneys. That's the made-up part."

By now, Marvin had reached back and was stroking Sammy's dick, which was springing back to life.

"Every year, Nick ... by the way, that is Santa's real name ... and I seek out a few individuals who have come into rough times and try to bring them some joy in the season. I have watched you since you were a child, always caring about other people, sacrificing your own happiness for others. You took care of your grandmother when she became ill with Alzheimer's and took her into your home, and you gave up your life for her. I knew your roommate didn't move out a while ago as you said. Your grandmother stayed in that room. Your grandmother died. While she was alive, your career suffered, but you didn't care as she was more important since she raised you after your parents died when you were a little boy," Marvin said as he looked at Sammy, who had tears in his eyes. "You took me in when you saw where I was living even though I was so mean to you these past few weeks."

"Was this a test?" Sammy asked as he placed his hands on Marvin's muscular thighs.

"Actually no," Marvin said. "You weren't going to be my subject this season. I was actually looking out for David, the store manager, but his heart is cold and made of stone."

"So why were you crying earlier?"

Marvin looked away for a second, but his hand stayed on Sammy's now rock-hard dick. "Because I was so focused on David, I didn't realize how bad things had become for you since your grandmother's death. While you were puttering around in your bedroom and I was unpacking my things, I sneaked a look at your checkbook. You have only eight dollars to your name."

Sammy turned away in shame, but Marvin reached up with his free hand and turned his face toward him. "Sammy, you have nothing to be ashamed of. I have spent three thousand years looking for someone like you to join Nick and me as we seek out those needing help and understanding. If you let me 'join with you,' you will be able to join us and become 'one of the just,' who gets to pick 'the chosen'."

Sammy looked confused. "What do you mean join with me then join with you? Will I become like you? Like a vampire, the undead?"

Marvin laughed, and his whole body shook like a bowl of gefilte fish in jellied broth.

"What is so funny?"

"Sammy, you read too many horror novels. No, you will not live forever. You will live a regular life, but that life will be far from normal, as you will have a purpose and you will spread *simchas* and *nachas* to those who need it," Marvin said with a twinkle in his eyes. "So, shall we join in this purpose?"

"Sure," Sammy answered without hesitation.

Marvin then slid down Sammy's body until he was between his legs. He then lifted Sammy's legs until they rested on his shoulders.

"Aren't you going to use some lube?" Sammy asked as he attempted to reach into the vanity.

"No need, my cock will provide enough eggnog to make this very pleasurable," Marvin said with a wink, and he aimed his recharged dick, which he stroked a few times to coat with the copious amounts of precum that was leaking from it, and aimed it at Sammy's hole.

"Wait ... what am I doing? I'm not a bottom!" Sammy exclaimed.

"You are now," Marvin said and drove his big cock in to the root without hesitation.

Sammy, who had braced himself for the pain, felt no pain, only bliss as Marvin proceeded to hump him for points. It only took a few minutes for them to come in unison, and it was the second hands-free orgasm of the night for Sammy. He shot so far that he hit his own face, and as he licked his lips, he marveled at how his own cum now tasted like ... like ... peppermint!

THE EDGE OF OBSESSION

I had waited a long time for this.

David had been the object of my affections for years, several years. I first saw his profile on Bigmuscle right after I joined up. I don't know why I became obsessed with him. Maybe it was the fact that he would tease me; say he would call; sometimes call; say he would go out with me; had dinner with me once; say he meant to call me.

We would run into each other on the street, and he would give me that "I could eat you for dinner look." He would tell me he would call. I would tell him I erased his number from my phone because I had given up on him. He would smile, wink, then promise to call. A month or two later, he would. Then nothing.

This went on for almost a decade. I don't know why. In that time, I dated other guys, got plenty of action, but I continued to obsess over David. It wasn't like he was something all that special. He was cute – very cute – a prematurely-gray haired Italian who was five-four if he was an inch, compact with just the right amount of muscle, and a smile that would melt your heart, or at least mine.

He was the opposite of me. I stood one foot taller, still had more black than gray hair, hardly compact but muscular nonetheless. David, you wanted to squeeze and cuddle. Me? Well, I had been described as intimidating, imposing, pushy, loud, etc. I am not the guy you want to squeeze. I am the guy you want to fuck. I am also the guy you want to throw you down and fuck you into the next zip code.

The problem is I am not really any of those things. I look like those things, but I am just a big, furry, Italian Teddy bear. And, this was the problem. David was probably scared of what would happen if he did end up in the bedroom with me. Little did he know.

# # # # #

I am still trying to figure out how it happened. As I said, it had been over a decade of trying. I remember running into him at a Pride festival in Annapolis of all places. We had our usual flirty chat, then he went on his way while I continued to staff our booth. Around five, or was it six, what does it matter? We were breaking down when he walked up to me and told me that his friend who drove him there left with a trick and would I be able to drive him back to town. I no longer lived in the city, so I told him I could drive him to my home and put him on the Metro from there. You see I drove my 1953 Willys Aero that day, and I didn't want to drive it into the city on a Saturday night.

Off we went.

We talked a bunch of nonsense in the car, and for once, I didn't flirt or even intimate that I wanted him to come inside. He offered to help me bring all the booth decorations into my house, and I didn't refuse.

Once we were done, I offered to walk him the two blocks to the Metro, and he said he would rather just hang out a bit. I said that was cool, but after standing in the heat for nine hours, I needed a shower, so I gave him the remote and walked back to the bathroom to shower.

I was facing the showerhead, rinsing the last of the soap from my face when I felt a hand on my waist that moved to my stomach, then down to my crotch and another hand reach between my legs and grab my balls. Needless to say I was hard in an instant.

After a decade of waiting, I was also ready to shoot in an instant, so I turned around quickly. He had that smile on his face that always got me. I grabbed the soap and proceeded to lather him up all over. Then I rinsed him off. We never said a word.

I handed him a towel, and we dried ourselves off in silence. Then, I led him into the bedroom. I picked him up and placed him on his back on the bed. I then straddled him, reached down beside the bed and grabbed four restraints, and before he know it, he was bound at all four corners.

I expected him to fight me off, but he had a look of trust in his eyes.

I bent down, brushed my lips over his and whispered, "You trust me. I can tell. Just relax. I am going to give you pleasure like you never had before." I then softly kissed him and gently let him have my tongue. He was extremely receptive, and when I ran my hand down that sexy torso, I found a nice hard cock waiting for me.

I stroked it lightly, and when I rolled my thumb over the tip and gathered a good amount of precum, I brought to our lips, and we both savored the taste. By now, I was generating quite a bit myself. Between the two of us, there was enough to generously lubricate our cocks, and lubricate them I did. I rubbed them together, and he started moaning and streaming more and more of the tasty stuff.

I then licked his neck slowly and worked my way down his sternum. My hand continued to stroke us gently and both our cocks were hard and throbbing with pleasure.

I licked my way over to his nipple, and he shuddered when I found it. I gently tugged with my teeth then worked my way to his left armpit. I love armpits, and his were sexy as hell. I licked and he loved it. I felt his cock harden even more, and I realized he was going to shoot, so I let go of our cocks. He whimpered.

I then ran my tongue over to the other side, grazing the right nipple on the way then tasting his right armpit.

I placed my hand on his cock again and found a puddle of precum on his belly. I used that and mine, which was dripping all over his cock and balls, to stroke us again. By now, he was writhing on the bed. Again, he was getting close, so I halted the stroke. He whimpered.

My tongue was back on his neck, and I worked my way up his throat. Once my mouth found his again, I slipped my tongue in. He tried to go for a heavy bit of making out, but I was in control and kept it gentle and delicate. This drove him wild. His cock was on fire, and the precum was flowing like syrup.

He whimpered as I left his mouth and worked my way down his torso again. I made a slow and steady trail with my tongue to his navel and oh so sexy belly. I love a muscleman's belly. There was also plenty of love juice on his belly to lap up, and lap it up I did.

I then found the tip of his cock with my mouth, and I gently sucked on it. He whimpered.

Then I took it all in, slowly, but steadily, and it pulsed in my mouth, so I slowed my suck to a crawl, so to speak.

"Let me come."

It was the first words he had spoken.

I released his cock, looked into his eyes and winked.

He whimpered.

I then proceeded to lick down his left leg. There is nothing sexier than a compact muscle guy's legs – except for every other part of him. He was just delicious. When I got to his foot, I looked up, and his dick was just as hard, and I wasn't touching it anymore. I took one toe into my mouth and sucked on it. He whimpered. I then tasted all his toes very slowly.

I still had not made a sound. This was all about him. But, my cock was hard and making a mess or precum on my floor. I didn't care. I had him where I wanted him.

I then worked my way up his right leg after savoring those toes for a long time.

I didn't know how much time had passed, but I guessed maybe an hour or so.

I reached his crotch and took one full ball in my mouth, and his cock jumped. He whimpered. Then I took both balls in my mouth, while my hands gently stroked his thighs.

I released his balls after getting them good and wet and licked up the length of his throbbing cock. I knew it must hurt from being hard so long. I know mine did.

I found the head all wet with precum and a huge puddle on that sexy belly again. I licked it all up then took his cock in my mouth again. He whimpered.

By now, my hands were working his balls, and my mouth was gently stroking his cock while my tongue found that sweet spot where the head meets the shaft. You know that spot where all the nerve endings meet.

He yelled, "Oh God."

He shot.

I swallowed.

I shot without touching myself.

I licked him clean.

He thanked me.

I untied him and gave him directions to the Metro.

He refused to leave.

I was happy.

THE EX

I decided to go to the gym early that day, a Sunday, so I figured the place would be empty. I changed in the locker room, and when I emerged, who would be standing at the front desk but my ex.

We had not seen each other in over a year – since he moved to Minneapolis. What the hell was he doing here, now? Why was he back in town?

"Hey, sexy," he greeted me.

"What are you doing in town?" I asked.

"Here on business." Then, he leaned into me and said, "And, I am horny as hell."

"That's nice," I replied and went upstairs to the workout floor. I really was not in the mood for his bullshit.

I did my workout and spotted him on the treadmill for a second, but I was also proud of myself for not caring one bit that he was there. It took me a long time to get over him, and I finally was.

After an hour, I had lifted all I cared to lift, and I went back downstairs to the locker room to shower.

I brushed my teeth (I don't know why working out gives me a bad taste in my mouth), stripped out of my sweaty gear, grabbed a towel and entered the shower room. Mine is an old fashioned gym with an open shower room. Being it was early Sunday morning, I and about two or three other people were actually in the gym, so the shower room was empty.

I was soaping up and had closed my eyes for a second when I heard, "Man, you are looking hot as ever."

There he was, under the shower head next to mine, in his hairy, muscular glory, with that thick cock just hanging there, as I fondly remembered it.

"Thanks," I muttered and proceeded to soap myself up.

"How's life?" he asked.

"Good," I answered as I was not really in the mood for conversation. I just wanted to clean up and get on with my day.

"Not much for talking today are you?" he said. Then he placed a soapy hand on my cock.

I didn't stop him, nor did I get hard.

"You usually harden up right away," he said as he used his other hand to cup my balls.

Then I started to get hard. Damn motherfucker, he knew how to get me up.

I pulled away.

"Really don't want to go there," I said. "It took me a long time to get over you, so let's not fuck things up, OK?"

He nodded. "No problem. I just like touching you and wouldn't mind having that up my ass right now." He winked.

I smiled at him as if he were a petulant child.

"I'm staying at the hotel next door. My flight leaves at noon, so I have an hour to kill."

"How long have you been in town?" I asked as if I cared.

"About a week."

Now, the old me would have said something to the effect of 'you've been here all week and you didn't call.' But, I was beyond that.

"I should have called."

"Why?" I asked.

He just looked at me then my dick, which had gone down a bit.

"Wow. You really do move on."

"Yep," I answered.

I finished my shower, grabbed my towel and exited the shower room.

He finished up then opened his locker, which turned out to be next to mine.

I dressed. He dressed. I said a quick goodbye and exited the gym. No sooner had the door closed behind me then it opened again.

"Fuck me now," he said to me from behind as I turned to walk down the street. "I am right next door, just take me and fuck me."

I turned and looked right at him. Should I fuck him? Would it bring back old feelings? Would this be a mistake? Could I do this and walk away again?

"What the hell," I said and followed him up to his hotel room.

No reason for pretense, we already saw each other naked in the shower room, we were together for over three years. No mystery there. We were naked in seconds.

I grabbed the bottle of lube that was on the night stand, greased up my hard pole pushed him back on the bed, lifted up his legs, aimed my dick, and entered swiftly.

He didn't even grimace, or yelp; he just smiled.

He put his hands behind his head and flexed his biceps. His dick was rock-hard and throbbing on his belly, and I was pounding him into the next time zone. He knew flexing his biceps would make me even harder. His kissed one then the other, while his hot, big, hairy ass swallowed my dick.

I fucked for points. I was determined to get off in him and fuck him until he begged me to stop. It takes me a long time to come, so he was in for a real long ride.

I leaned down and kissed him. Long and hard, we wrestled tongues, then he stuck his out, and I sucked on his tongue while I continued to drill him.

He was in heaven. What a bottom slut he was. His dick was dribbling all over his belly, and he was still flexing those baseball-sized biceps and smiling like a fat kid eating cake.

I don't know how long I fucked him. I just kept going and going. This was better than cardio. Finally, I knew I was going over the edge, and I looked right at him, right in the eyes.

"I am going to seed your guts," I said low and with a growl. And, I emptied my balls into him and continued to pound him until he let out a moan and came without touching himself.

I pulled out.

"I need a shower," I announced, then walked into the bathroom, turned on the water, and stepped in.

This is when he would usually join me. He didn't, and I was glad. I cleaned my dick, then took a long piss in the shower. I stepped out, grabbed a towel, and looked in the trash can. There were two empty Fleet Enema bottles. Miserable slut cleaned himself out, knowing he would get fucked this morning. Nothing changed. And, that is when I knew even fucking him wouldn't make me love him again.

I dressed and said goodbye.

I never gave him another thought. As a matter of fact, by lunchtime, I had forgotten I had even fucked him.

DUDE, IT WAS JUST A BLOW JOB

Sometimes being horny can get you into a situation that you find isn't worth the mind-blowing orgasm you experienced.

OK, it wasn't mind-blowing, but it satisfied a need.

There I was walking my dog when this hot older man, a kind of daddy type, stopped to pet my dog, and chatted me up.

He offered me a blowjob.

I accepted.

I told him where I lived and to give me thirty minutes, so we could finish our walk, and I could shower.

He knocked on my door exactly thirty minutes later. I answered wearing nothing but sweat pants. I showed him to the bedroom, dropped my sweats and lay down on my back. I told him to strip, and for a sixty-year-old (or even a forty-year-old), he had a pretty nice body.

He climbed between my legs and proceeded to give me one of the best blowjobs of my life. He told me what a perfect dick I had, and how it tasted so good, and all that other bullshit you hear in bed.

He worked me good, and I shot in his mouth.

He didn't swallow. Instead, he ran into the bathroom and spit it out in the sink. Then, he washed his mouth out with soap.

That was a total turn-off. I would rather he let me shoot on myself than attempt to swallow.

He smiled asked if he could do it again sometime, and I said yes. He was on his way.

It was just a blowjob.

I then got an email from him. Somehow, he found me on Facebook. He told me how hot I was, and how he hoped I wasn't freaked out. He wanted me to feel comfortable. He went on and on about feelings and God knows what. He offered to do me again.

I emailed back. "Dude, it was just a blowjob."

We ran into each other on the street a few days later. He told me how he wanted to blow me again. I said I was busy, but maybe some other time. He continued wherever he was going. I went home.

He emailed me later that day saying how I shouldn't get so uncomfortable when I see him on the street, and he found me so attractive and wanted to suck my dick again.

I emailed back, "Dude, it was just a blowjob."

Later that week, there was a knock on my door. I looked through the peep hole. It was Daddy BJ.

He asked if I was horny. I politely asked that he not drop by again. I said it was nothing personal, but I wasn't in the mood.

He pulled out a gun. He pointed it at my chest. He pulled the trigger. I fell to the ground. He looked at me. I mumbled back, "Dude, it was just a blowjob."

And everything went black.

STEPBROTHERS

With spring semester over, Adam headed home for the summer before his senior year at State University. His mother had remarried in the last month, and she and her new husband were still on their honeymoon, so Adam knew he was coming home to an empty house.

After a three-hour drive, he was happy to be pulling up in front of the house, and he noticed the hatchback parked in the driveway and figured it must belong to one of his new stepfather's kids, probably checking on the house.

Adam pulled his suitcases out of the trunk and walked up the walkway, let himself in, and walked right up the stairs. After a long drive, he was in no mood to talk to anyone.

He put the suitcases in his room, and the first thing he noticed was how hot it was in the house. If one of his new step siblings was there, why didn't he turn on the AC? Adam shook his head and took off his shirt.

Adam had been lifting weights since he was sixteen. His body was perfectly proportioned and nicely muscled at five-foot-eleven and 185 pounds. He inherited his mother's smooth chocolate brown skin and his father's large round ass, among other large assets.

He walked downstairs to turn on the air conditioning. While adjusting the thermostat, he heard the front door open and someone saying goodbye, followed by a car speeding away. He remembered his stepbrother from the wedding. Louis was a little taller than Adam at six-foot-one, but he was leaner. His nineteen-year-old stepbrother had thick black curly hair and very dark features much like his father's, with black eyes and thick lips that begged to be kissed.

Adam remembered talking to him at the wedding and wondering if it would be incestuous to lay his new stepbrother.

"Hey, Adam," Louis said as he extended his hand. The two of them shook hands.

"Dude, what's with not turning on the AC? It's like a fucking oven in here," Adam said.

Louis shook his head and headed upstairs. That was when Adam remembered that Louis was not much of a talker, and from what he gathered from his mother and Louis's siblings, he was not always playing with a full deck either.

Nutty or not, Adam still wondered if the boy liked to play.

He headed back to his bedroom and unpacked his bags. After putting away the last of his clothes and putting the suitcases in the closet, he headed back downstairs to the kitchen for some water. His mother always kept a large jug of water in the refrigerator, and he decided to forgo a glass and drink it straight from the jug. As he was guzzling the water, Louis walked into the kitchen.

"Adam, the man," he said.

Adam quit guzzling for a second and looked at Louis who had stripped to his boxers. The boy was long and lean, built like a swimmer with broad shoulders and a six pack. This pissed Adam off because he knew Louis never worked out, but he did hold out hope that Louis would end up fat when he hit thirty!

"So, Louis, are you living here now, or are you house sitting?" Adam asked him.

"Wouldn't you like to know, bro," Louis said, and he grabbed a soda and headed back to his room.

Adam rolled his eyes and finished the jug. He filled it with tap water, put it back in the fridge and hoped it was full of bacteria for Louis to enjoy.

Adam headed upstairs, walked into the bathroom, stripped and stepped into the shower. While he was soaping up, he thought of Louis, the weirdo, standing in the kitchen wearing nothing but his boxers, and his dick started to grow. Adam had not come in a few days, so he took hold of his favorite toy and rubbed out a big load, barely taking a couple of minutes to do the deed, and hardly making a sound in the process as he learned to stay quiet while jerking off in the dorm.

He finished his shower and pulled the curtain back, grabbing a towel at the same time. Adam was startled to find Louis there flossing his teeth. The house had two full baths, why was he in this one?

Adam tried his best to conceal his cock, which was still half hard. It was difficult enough to hide when it was soft. However, Louis paid no attention to him, so Adam thought he would take one more stab at conversation.

"So, Louis, are you working or going to school?"

Louis stopped flossing and turned around to look at Adam, who had since wrapped the towel around his waist. Then he faced the mirror again.

"No," Louis said. He finished flossing and went into the guest room, shutting the door behind him.

"What a doofus," Adam said to himself. "I hope the little asshole isn't here all summer."

Adam brushed his teeth then crawled into bed.

At three in the morning, Adam was startled awake by some strange sounds. He thought there were cats fucking outside his window, but he soon realized the sounds were coming from the next room. He heard squeaking, then high pitched moaning, more squeaking, and then Louis's voice saying over and over again, "Good boy, good boy, good boy."

Adam never heard anyone come in. Who the hell was Louis talking to? Then he heard him yell, "AHHH AHHH AHHH," so loudly it shook the walls. Adam buried his head in his pillow to keep from laughing. Once the screaming stopped, he then heard Louis saying, "I am such a good boy, oh yeah, good boy, good boy." Then, there was silence.

Adam was still laughing as he thought about his strange stepbrother masturbating and congratulating himself. Then he got hard again, himself, but he was too tired to jerk off, so he rolled over and went back to sleep.

Adam woke up early the next morning and decided to make himself a pot of coffee and work out in the basement gym, provided it was still there. After locating his extra large mug, he filled it with the freshly brewed coffee and headed to the basement.

Since it was still pretty early, Adam decided to work out in just a black cotton jock strap, crew socks and cross trainers. The jock hugged his round butt and displayed his big basket perfectly, and he wished there were someone there to enjoy the view.

Once in the basement, he was happy to see that for the most part his equipment was still where he left it.

He loaded a couple of plates on the bar and secured them with collars. He decided to stretch a bit, and when he bent down to touch his toes he looked through his legs and saw Louis, stark naked and standing right behind him. Adam immediately stood up and turned around.

Louis was standing there with his dick hanging limp but low accompanied by two big, equally low hanging balls, and he was holding a cup of coffee.

"Adam, the man," Louis said. "I took some of your aromatic java." He then turned around and headed back upstairs.

Adam was only pissed because he would now have to brew more coffee.

He slid under the bar and pressed the weights for twelve reps, and he sat up after the set and admired himself in the mirror he had mounted across from the bench. Adam ran his hands over his chest and down his six pack abs. He then flexed both biceps, displaying the high peaks that always earned him attention in the gym at school.

He lay back down and did another twelve reps. With each set, he looked in the mirror and flexed his pecs, bouncing them before doing another double bicep pose.

Adam stood up and removed some of the plates and curled the barbell for ten reps very slowly, keeping his eyes on the vein that ran up his arm. Watching his biceps pump full of blood always turned him on, and his jock was beginning to get tighter.

He put the bar down, and flexed again, doing a crab pose, flaring out his lats and finishing off with another double bicep pose. Adam then did another set of curls.

During his third set, he heard Louis coming down the steps. Adam finished the set and put the bar back. This time Louis was sitting in front of the mirror drinking another cup of coffee, blocking Adam's view of himself. 'Fucking asshole,' he thought, 'Drinks my coffee and interrupts my workout.' However, Adam didn't confront him because Louis was still naked.

"Can I help you, Louis?" he asked.

Silence.

Louis just stared at Adam, studying every inch of him. Adam noticed how Louis was looking at him and didn't know what to make of it.

"Louis, you're sitting in front of the mirror, and I can't watch myself when I work out."

Louis turned and looked at the mirror as if he did not know it was there. He stood up and leaned on an old dresser that was placed in the basement a decade before.

"Louis, are you just going to stand there?" Adam asked him.

Again, silence.

Adam did another set of curls, watching himself in the mirror when he noticed Louis standing behind him. Louis reached around and felt Adam's biceps with each curl of the bar, running his hands over the pumped muscles. Adam continued his set, enjoying the feel of his stepbrother's hands on his muscles, and he started to get hard again.

Adam curled until he was exhausted, then he put the bar back on the rack. As he looked at himself in the mirror, Louis continued to explore his body with his hands.

Louis felt his stepbrother's lats, tracing his fingers up Adam's muscular back, then he squeezed Adam's softball sized shoulders, and as one hand made its way up Adam's neck the other reached around to feel Adam's pumped chest.

As Louis continued exploring his body, Adam's breathing became heavier. He let his stepbrother enjoy every sweaty, pumped inch of him and finally, Louis's hand was inside the black cotton jock strap and going for the prize.

As he released his stepbrother's enormous boner, Louis stepped around and brushed his lips against Adam's. Adam opened his mouth and reached around Louis's head drawing him in and kissing him deep, tasting the coffee the asshole had taken without permission. With his free hand, Adam reached down and grabbed the weirdo's hard dick and was impressed with its length and girth. Adam slid his hand up to the swollen head and slicked it with the precum Louis's big dick generously provided.

Louis had managed to get Adam's jock down around his ankles, and they continued to make out while stroking each other's dicks. Louis's free hand continued to explore Adam's pumped body and found a nipple, giving it a hard pull. Adam moaned, but he did not let go of Louis's mouth. Those full, soft lips were too good to let loose even for a second.

He let go of Louis's head and flexed his right bicep while his stepbrother felt it with his left hand, as they continued to kiss. Louis obviously liked the feel of flexed muscles because his dick would swell and pulse, emitting more precum whenever Adam flexed. This in turn made Adam's thick cock swell up, and he didn't know how much longer he could last.

Their breathing increased, and the stepbrothers were getting closer, but they never unlocked their lips.

Finally, Louis pulled away from Adam's lips and screamed, "AHHH AHHH AHHH," so loud it startled Adam. Then he shot his load covering Adam's belly and chest with pints of cum. The site of his stepbrother's load on his pumped chest made Adam shoot all over Louis, who groaned while Adam was shooting, "You are such a good boy, oh yeah, good boy, good boy." Then, there was silence.

They pulled away from each other, and Adam grabbed a towel to wipe himself off, but Louis stopped him. He bent down and licked his stepbrother's body clean. After he finished his breakfast of cum, he winked at Adam, turned and walked back upstairs without saying a word.

Adam stood there with his half-hard cock hanging out and his black cotton jock at his ankles and watched Louis's round butt bounce as he walked upstairs.

"What a fucking nut job," Adam thought. Then he smiled and hoped all his workouts would end like this one.

SCRUBBING UP

I had just come home from a business trip and was still wound up from days of meetings and travel. Normally, I would have had a martini then crashed for the night, but I hadn't worked out in a few days, so I decided to hit the gym. It was after 10:30, but they were open until midnight on Friday nights, so I had plenty of time.

After changing into my nondescript workout gear as I never really went for the Spandex/Lycra look, I walked upstairs to the free weight area, and to my surprise, no one else was working out. Usually this would bother me as seeing hot guys pumping up is inspirational, but I just wanted to get a good sweat going.

After an hour of working my chest until I swore my nipples would pop off from the pressure, I did some crunches and decided to call it a night and go downstairs to the locker room and shower. Interestingly, no one else came in to work out while I was there, and from what I could tell, only the night manager remained on duty.

As I undressed at my locker, the manager walked by and smiled. I am usually a talkative guy, but I noticed a while back, that although he was friendly and smiled a lot, this particular manager wasn't much of a talker, so I never initiated conversation. He was also the kind that never went for me – buzz cut, tattoos from neck to ankles, earrings, and from what I could tell through his tight shirt, nipple rings. He was also the bodybuilder type with big, thick muscles that were obviously enhanced through chemistry (and I'll leave it at that). He did have those dark features I find enormously attractive, but his look told me that I was not his type.

I bent down to slip off my jock, and I stood up to find him standing in front of me and checking me out.

"Pretty slow tonight," he said.

"Yeah, made my workout that much easier." I didn't bother covering myself up with a towel, as by then he had a full view and what was the point. I am also very well built with a naturally smooth physique and slabs of lean, hard muscle from years of working out, so I like the attention. My dick hangs nicely, too, with a pair of round full balls to support it. This would have been a good time to put on the moves, but as I said, this type never goes for me. My being blond doesn't help either.

"I still have time to shower before you lock up I hope."

"You have plenty of time," he said as he walked away then shouted over his shoulder, "I'm going to lock up early, but take your time."

We have open showers, which I like because there is nothing better than having a hot view of pumped up muscle-heads after a workout, and I had picked up my share of tricks after a shower in this gym as well.

I stepped up to the second shower head that I knew had the best pressure, turned it on and let the water cascade down my back as I faced the wall. I then shampooed my hair and turned around to rinse out the suds. I almost jumped when I felt a hand on my balls. I opened my eyes to see the night manager, naked and feeling me up while grinning at me.

"Mind if I soap you up?"

I just shrugged as if to say what the hell. He then squeezed some soap from the dispenser and proceeded to rub the soap on my chest, down my abs, back up my sides and indicated I should raise my arms as he scrubbed my pits. We didn't say a word as he continued to soap me up from head to toe while I drank in every tattooed inch of muscle on his beautiful body. Not only were his nipples pierced, but his belly button and big, thick cock were as well. I was intrigued by his body art, turned on by his beauty, and getting horny from his touch. My cock was standing straight up, thick and long, and the head was more swollen than usual.

He turned me around and worked my back, paying special attention to my hard, round glutes before he worked his hand between them and stuck a finger in my hole while he reached around with the other hand and stroked my now-aching cock.

Then he licked the back of my neck. That did it. About a quart of precum oozed from my cock, but the water and soap disguised it, although my moan was loud and clear.

I then felt his hard cock sliding up and down my crack and the smooth metal of the ring tracing its path. What a feeling, and I didn't want it to end.

I hardly ever bottom, but he was doing things with his hands on my body that had me almost begging out loud. I know he sensed my desire because he then let the head of his cock slide between my cheeks and without stumbling, fumbling or mumbling, he found the hole.

Yes, he was an expert top – a rare breed and a fantastic find. The few times I ever bottomed, I got annoyed when they would struggle to find the hole and get to work, always thinking, 'Find it already, fuck me and leave.'

He penetrated me ever so gently but with a steady movement, and before I knew it, that hard, thick pierced tool was all the way in, and I oozed another quart of precum. The metal ring just added to my pleasure as doing me from behind allowed it to rub my prostate just right. He continued to lick my neck and stroke my cock while he fucked me slowly never increasing nor decreasing his pace. I was in heaven. And, I was getting close.

Within a minute, I shot with a loud growl and painted the tiles with my thick load while he continued his steady fuck. Once he was sure I was drained, he withdrew his cock, and I ached for its return. It was over, and I wanted it to go on all night. I was embarrassed at my quick orgasm, but he seemed not to mind.

He turned me around and proceeded to soap me up again as he did before, but this time he leaned in and planted his full lips on mine. Not only was he a great fuck, but also the best kisser I have ever known. My cock, which I thought was through for the night, got hard again (his stroking it didn't hurt).

This time instead of turning me around, he turned around and rubbed his big hard muscular ass on my cock. I got the message. I found the hole with no problem and penetrated him with the same gentle but firm steady stroke he had shown me. I ran my tongue up his back and all over his neck, while I reached around and stroked his cock. He moaned with pleasure as I fucked him steadily, figuring he liked it as he gave it, slow, steady, firm and sensual. I have learned from years of casual encounters that if someone does something to you, they usually like it done to them.

He liked it.

Within a minute, he growled out his own thick load and painted the tile floor.

Strangely, we had only been at it for no more than ten or fifteen minutes, yet we had both come and fucked each other. I could have come again, but I withdrew. I also decided to return the favor and scrub him up.

His body felt fantastic; the more I felt of it, the more I wanted to go at it again.

"Come home with me," he said.

Those were the first words either of us had spoken since he entered the shower.

"OK."

We rinsed off, and as I walked toward his car, I wondered what a guy like him wanted with a guy like me.

That was more than twenty years ago, but I no longer wonder what he sees in me as long as he fucks me slow and steady and lets me return the favor every night.

THE ONE GIVING
THE ORDERS

Another scorcher on Paris Island, South Carolina, and Master Sergeant Masters was ready to call it a day. Seven weeks into boot camp with the latest flock of recruits was taking its toll on Masters, and he swore after week eleven, once they were done with him and off to infantry training, he would retire. Twenty-five years he had spent in the Marines, and he was damn proud of his service to his country. Although he never saw combat, he had trained by last count over 11,000 recruits – the majority of whom arrived as long-haired pussies and left as jar-headed fighting machines.

His once deep resonating voice had matured to a prematurely raspy quality due to years of yelling orders and berating the greens.

After marching his boys into the barracks, he handed over control to Master Sergeant Earl, completed some paperwork, hopped into his Dodge pick-up, and drove to his home in Beaufort. He had chosen to live off base a few years before when he spotted the little house while out for some R&R one weekend. There was a for sale sign on it, and once he had contacted the real estate agent and taken a tour, he knew it was the home he always wanted. Having always lived modestly, driving an almost thirty-year-old truck at the time and always living on base, he was able to pay cash for the house with a little to spare to fix it up. His favorite feature was the basement. Basements were rare in these parts being so close to the coast, but this house was over 100 years old.

Masters pulled up to the house, parked his truck around back, and hopped out. He inspected his garden, then he stretched his arms and let out a roar. Barking orders all day had taken its toll, and at forty-six, he was getting seriously tired of always being in charge. Masters looked down at the garden and noticed some weeds popping up, so he started pulling them out. The sun was baking, so he pulled off his olive-green T-shirt, revealing his hairy, muscular torso. All he had on were his fatigues and boots. At six-feet even and over 225 pounds, Masters was a solid mountain of muscle. Prominent veins, which could be seen over the matt of salt and pepper hair on his arms, popped from his forearms up across his biceps right over his deltoids. His chest was two solid mounds of pectoral muscle covered in the same salt and pepper hair, which didn't conceal his large protruding nipples – nipples one just wanted to suck and chew on for hours. And, Masters wouldn't have minded that as they were hot-wired right to his gigantic dick.

He continued pulling the weeds and was working his way across the garden, when he heard a vehicle pull up in front of his house. He then heard a door open and shut, then another.

"What have we here?" came a voice at the foot of the garden.

Masters looked up and saw two men, both wearing fatigues and boots and no shirts standing there in his backyard looking at him. He recognized both of them. The man who had spoken was Private First Class Boneman, who finished boot camp a little over a year ago. Boneman was around five-foot-ten 170 pounds with light blond hair covering his young, muscular body, a handsome face with blue eyes and a blond high-and-tight haircut. Standing next to him was his boot camp buddy, Private First Class Firestone, who was considerably shorter than Boneman, but weighed the same, displaying a thickly muscled frame. The little man had dark features, smooth skin and hauntingly black eyes. One could tell immediately he was not the brightest guy, but sexy nonetheless.

"I think it's our favorite drill instructor, Master Sergeant Masters," Firestone answered.

Masters stared at the two boys, expressionless. He didn't know why they were here, nor did he care. Once the boys were done with boot camp, he was done with them.

"So, growing pretty flowers, Sarge?" Boneman asked as he walked toward Masters with Firestone beside him.

"What do you boys want?" Masters said as he stood up.

Instantly, Boneman lunged toward him while Firestone grabbed his arms and pinned them behind his back. Boneman held a hand at Masters' throat while he grabbed the top of his fatigues with the other hand.

"We're here to have a little fun with our favorite drill instructor," Boneman said as he spit in the sergeant's face.

Masters just stared him down.

Firestone removed his military-issue belt and tied Masters' wrists behind his back, and Boneman grabbed the older man's dog tags and led him into the house. They entered through the back door into the kitchen, where Boneman opened the first door he saw, which turned out to be a broom closet. He opened a second door, which opened to a staircase leading to the basement. After feeling inside the wall for a light switch and turning it on, he continued to lead Masters by the dog tags while Firestone held onto his bound wrists and pushed him from behind as they descended the stairs into the dimly lit basement.

"Woo hoo, lookey here," Boneman said as he scanned the room.

There was a sling hanging down in the middle of the room, off to one side was a wall with permanently attached restraints, a weight bench was situated in one corner, and in the opposite corner was a claw-type bathtub. Interestingly, hanging over the bath tub were chains with wrist restraints attached at the ends. Various brushes, hoses and other odds and ends were sitting on a table next to the tub.

"Get him into the tub!" Boneman barked at Firestone, who did as he was told. Masters tried to resist, but the little muscleman was still able to steer him over and into the tub. Boneman reached up and pulled down the two chains, removed the belt that Firestone had used, while the little man held onto the sergeant's wrists. Boneman grabbed one of his wrists, brought it in front of him, and restrained it on the chain then he did the same with the other. He then pulled the chains up, so Masters' hands were above his head.

Boneman looked him in the eyes, and when he did, Masters spit in his face. Boneman wiped the spit from his face then punched Masters in the gut, which to the young man's surprise was like a brick wall. The feel of the older man's rock- hard abs against his fist sent a shockwave to Boneman's crotch, and he punched him again. Three more punches, and his dick was drooling. Masters only grunted with each punch, being no stranger to pain.

"Get his boots and pants off!" Boneman ordered the little man.

Firestone did as he was told, and when Masters tried to resist, Boneman punched him again.

Masters was now standing in the tub only wearing his olive green boxers, which Boneman wasted no time ripping off him.

"Hey Firestone, look at that?" Boneman said as he scanned the big naked man in front of him. "What do you think, eight, nine, maybe even ten?" he continued while pointing to the older man's dick, which was flaccid but hanging a good seven thick inches nonetheless.

"Those hairy balls are as big as apples," Firestone chimed in. "Pretty impressive for a girl with a flower garden."

Boneman chuckled at the little muscleman's joke then he ran his hand down Masters' body, feeling the salt and pepper hair and then grabbing his nuts, which barely fit in his hand. Masters' dick started to grow with Boneman's handling of his sack.

"Clean him out," Boneman said to Firestone, while still holding the sergeant by the short hairs.

"With what?" Firestone asked dumbly.

Boneman reluctantly let go of the balls and grabbed the hose that was attached to the faucet. It was a chrome hose with a narrow spray attachment at the end, shaped too much like an enema.

"With this ... I'll loosen the chains, so he can be on all fours in the tub," Boneman said as he handed the hose to Firestone.

Boneman loosened the chains and guided Masters down, so he was now on all fours with his big, hairy, muscular ass in the air. The sight of the sergeant's hairy hole up in the air was almost enough to make Boneman cream his fatigues, and one look at Firestone's pants confirmed that he also appreciated the view.

Boneman turned the tap on lukewarm, and Firestone inserted the hose into the sergeant's hairy hole, and the drill instructor didn't even flinch, for he didn't want them to have the pleasure of knowing how much they were humiliating him.

"Fill him up. I want him clean before I go in there," Boneman said with a smile.

"The hell you will!" Masters protested, speaking for the first time since entering the basement.

Boneman leaned down, cupped Masters' chin and said, "Did I ask you to speak? You aren't in charge here. I am. Maybe it's time you learned to take orders rather than give them. You got that, you miserable motherfucker?"

"Yes, Sir," the sergeant mumbled.

"I didn't hear you, pussy!" Boneman barked.

"Sir, Yes, Sir!" Masters bellowed as his bowels were filled with the warm water.

Firestone removed the hose, and Boneman told him to push. As the water sprayed from his aching hole, it was not as clear as Boneman would have preferred.

"Do it again, and keep doing it until it's clean enough to drink," Boneman told Firestone.

And, again, Firestone inserted the hose. After five times with the hose and evacuating on command, the water was crystal clear, and Firestone used the hose to spray the excess water down the drain.

"Now, we'll get him all cleaned up ... the same way he used to order us to clean up that stinky recruit with a scrub brush ... what was his name?" Boneman asked.

Firestone answered, "Robert Taylor."

"Yeah."

Boneman removed the enema attachment from the hose and attached a garden sprayer, while Firestone removed his own boots, pants and boxers, then put his boots back on, revealing his own hefty meat, which was secured with a leather cock ring, making his full balls swell.

"I don't want to get wet ... man I got to take a piss," Fireman said, while handling his prick.

"Take a piss then, just be sure you aim for his face," Boneman said as he removed his own clothes.

Firestone then positioned himself in front of the sergeant and released a healthy stream of his urine all over Masters' face and hair, while the sergeant just closed his eyes. Boneman noticed how the older man opened his mouth slightly to taste the nasty stream and chuckled at what a pig the man was. Boneman then put his boots back on, and marveled that Firestone was still pissing, when he decided to join in and released a healthy stream from his own thick meat, which was supported with a chrome cock ring, all over Masters' face and hair. When they were done emptying their bladders and shook the last drops on the older man, Boneman turned on the hose and sprayed down the drill instructor starting with his hair and working his way back to his well worked over hole. He then handed the hose to Firestone, while he pulled the chains bringing the man to a standing position again.

When the two young men looked down, they saw that the sergeant's dick was standing at half-mast and a good ten inches in front of him.

"I knew it would get huge," Boneman said to Firestone, who whistled. "Now scrub him down."

Firestone sprayed the water into a bucket that was next to the tub, filled it with the liquid soap that was on the table, grabbed the scrub brush, and dipped it into the sudsy water. He then started with Masters' head, which was a reach for the shorter of the two men, and worked his way down Masters' entire body until he was covered in suds and clean enough for inspection. Boneman then rinsed the suds off with quite a hard setting on the sprayer, yet

Masters refused to acknowledge even the slightest pain or humiliation.

"He's a tough old fart," Boneman said as he turned off the faucet.

"A hot one, too," Firestone said. But, Boneman gave him an angry look for saying anything positive about the older man.

"Let's get him over to the sling," Boneman ordered as he undid the restraints on Masters' wrists. "And if you try anything, you'll be sorry, old man," he said as he looked Masters in the eye, and again Masters spit in his face. Boneman immediately followed with another punch to his stomach. He then punched him two more times, and his own dick reacted at the feeling of the sergeant's rock-hard abs against his fist.

With the position of authority firmly established, they marched Masters over to the sling, lifted him into it, and secured his wrists and ankles, so he was on his back with his powerful legs spread. Surprisingly, the drill instructor's cock got even harder once he was restrained, and almost reached its full eleven by seven inches, when Boneman clamped two clothespins on Masters' large hot-wired nipples. Boneman grabbed the huge dick, gave it a good squeeze, and said, "Too bad you're such a bottom pussy, motherfucker."

Firestone's thick seven-inch cock was standing straight up at this point as he awaited his next order, and Boneman's eight inches were almost at full staff, too.

"Bring me that tin container over there," Boneman ordered as he pointed to the table of supplies. "And that black rubber glove, too."

Masters' eyes popped open.

Boneman looked right at him, and said, "I want to see if my fist'll fit up this big hairy hole of yours. Think you can take it, old man?"

Masters didn't answer, but gave him a look that practically said, "I'll kill you when this is all over with."

Firestone brought over the tin container and the black rubber glove and stood there watching as Boneman picked up the glove, then discarded it, and then opened up the container, scooping a handful of white grease into his right hand. He then slathered it liberally over his hand before he aimed for the sergeant's hole. He dispensed with pleasantries and decided to begin with two fingers, and the sergeant grunted for the first time, acknowledging the intrusion.

"What do you want me to do?" Firestone asked dumbly.

"How about you keep him quiet."

"How?"

"Stick that thick cock of yours in his mouth ... that should shut him up," Boneman suggested.

Firestone then positioned himself at Masters' head and grabbed his face, opened the older man's mouth and stuffed his stiff rod clear down to the hilt. He then fucked the sergeant's face with long, slow strokes, enjoying the warm feeling.

"Careful he doesn't bite the head off. If he tries, just punch him in the face," Boneman told his buddy.

Boneman then inserted a third finger, and Masters' dick twitched, and his groan was muffled, but he didn't clamp down on the thick meat he was sucking. Firestone kept up his rhythm as Boneman inserted another finger, making it four total. Again, Masters groaned, and Firestone's eyes rolled up. Boneman noticed Firestone's expression and barked, "Don't come yet, dumb ass, I'm just getting started."

Boneman rolled his four fingers around, loosening up the hairy muscular hole, and slowly introduced his thumb. With that, Masters muffled a scream or was it a yell, and with Firestone's cock now resting in his mouth rather than pumping as he was trying to hold off, one couldn't tell. But, Boneman was not done. He then slowly worked his fist into the ass of his former drill instructor, and with a slow but steady motion, worked it all the way in, past his wrist and almost halfway up his forearm. Boneman's cock released a long stream of precum that dangled to the floor; Firestone's eyes lit up at the sight of his buddy's arm up Masters' asshole; and Masters' eyes rolled up as his dick started to swell then twitch rapidly.

Firestone lost it first as the sight before him and the mouth on his hot cock was too much for the horny little muscleman. His cock shot a hefty load into the sergeant's mouth that the older man eagerly swallowed without missing a drop. And, that was enough to send Masters over the edge as the fist up his ass, the clothespins on his nipples, and the sweet load in his mouth made his eleven-inch cock twitch violently until he came clear up to his neck without even touching himself.

There was a lot of panting as Firestone removed his cock from Masters' mouth, and Boneman was the only one who still had full balls.

"Damn, did I give anyone permission to come!" Boneman yelled.

"Fuck you, prick," Masters said.

With that Boneman removed his fist from the sergeant's ass, walked over to the side of the sling, and punched him repeatedly in the stomach, which wasn't easy considering Masters was still in a supine position. Again, the rock hard abs against his fist turned Boneman on, and as he felt the load work its way out of his balls and up the length of his cock, he grabbed it and aimed for Masters' face, releasing a load that was heftier than the two released by the other men.

"Now, who's the prick, motherfucker?" Boneman said as he shook the last of his spunk out of his still-raging cock and onto the older man's mouth.

Masters just looked at him and smiled. Boneman let out a little grin also, and Firestone couldn't control himself any longer, saying, "Fuck, that was hot."

"Damn, if you don't stop breaking scene, Firestone, I am gonna stick my whole foot up your ass!" Boneman said, almost seriously.

"Promise?" Firestone asked with a smile.

# # # # #

After cleaning up, the three men were sitting in Masters' living room drinking a few beers and finishing one of the three pizzas they ordered. They were all wearing nothing but their boxers, and the pizza delivery guy had given them a curious look, but seeing the muscles on the three men, decided not to say anything, just collect his money and leave.

"So, how long to retirement?" Boneman asked.

"Four weeks," Masters answered as he took a swig of his beer.

"We'll be in Afghanistan by then," Firestone said with a sorrowful look.

Masters looked at the two young men he had trained not too long ago, and he felt a heaviness in his heart at the thought of them going off to war, but he was not one to get sentimental, at least not outwardly. He also silently prayed they would be OK and be able to see him again when they returned.

"Man have I got to take a piss," Masters announced as he stood up.

Firestone looked at him, then at Boneman, and got up from the couch and walked to the bathroom. Masters followed him, and Boneman did the same. When they arrived in the bathroom, Firestone was in the tub, naked and leaning on the wall.

Without saying a word, Masters dropped his boxers, whipped out his monster meat and aimed for the little muscleman, covering him with his hot stream. Boneman, positioned himself beside the sergeant, dropped his own boxers, put his arm around Masters' waist and added to Firestone's golden shower. Boneman then looked up at the sergeant, who then looked down at him and planted his mouth on the young jarhead's, driving his tongue inside and enjoying the taste of beer and pizza while they continued spraying their buddy, who by now was stroking his cock at the sight before him and the feeling of warm piss all over him.

WHO'S THE DADDY?

Wayne left work his usual time and drove home not thinking about much of anything. Lately, he had been in a funk. He didn't know why. His career was going great. He was in a happy loving relationship with a hot man twenty years his junior, and although he was fifty-five years old, he had the body of a man in his twenties. Wayne was over six-feet tall with 200 pounds of silver-fur covered muscle and a tight bubble-butt that would be the envy and desire of any man at any age. But, even with all he had going for him, he sighed as he pulled into the driveway.

He opened the front door and looked down to see his thirty-five-year-old partner, Marty, on all fours in the living room wearing nothing but a dog collar, a leash and a leather cock ring. Wayne looked at him and gave a faint smile. Normally, he would be up for some puppy play, but he couldn't muster the energy to train his dog today.

Wayne walked past the living room into the kitchen and opened the refrigerator. Marty stood up and followed him. Marty was four inches taller and had twenty-five more pounds of muscle than Wayne, and the cock ring only added to the allure of his long, thick cock and heavy balls. He had dark features and jet black hair, and his body was smooth with just a touch of black hair in between his mountainous pecs that trailed down to his thick black pubic hair. He kept his huge balls shaved smooth, and Wayne kept Marty's crack shaved smooth as well, for he preferred it that way.

"Don't you want to play with me?" Marty asked as he licked Wayne's neck.

Wayne shrugged away. "I'm sorry, Babe, another time. I'm just not in the mood right now." He closed the refrigerator door after grabbing a beer, looked at Marty and grabbed the younger man's balls. "It's not you. It could never be you."

Marty's cock responded as it always did to Wayne's touch, but he knew that this was not the time to push his partner – or beg. Wayne released his balls and turned to look out the kitchen window while drinking his beer.

They had been together for over ten years, and each knew the other better than the back of his own hand. They knew when the other was not in the mood, and neither would push or whine just to play, probably because they played almost all the time and rarely were not in the mood. And, play they did – from puppy play to water sports, fisting, light bondage, heavy bondage, ball torture – you name it. But, no matter how they played, Wayne was always the dominant one, and Marty the submissive, and they took to their roles with relish.

Marty turned from the kitchen and went upstairs to change. A less secure partner would be hurt by the rejection, but Marty knew Wayne was in a funk. The problem was this funk seemed to last longer than usual as they had not played in over a week – an eternity for them. He went into the bedroom, took off the collar and cock ring and put on a pair of sweatpants. Wayne entered the bedroom as Marty was tying the drawstring. He walked up to him, put his hand on the back of his head and kissed him long and hard. Again, Marty's cock responded. Wayne released his lips from Marty and looked down at the hefty bulge.

"God, you're a sexy motherfucker," he said to Marty with a smile.

Marty smiled back at him and said, "Why don't you go out tonight? Maybe you need to get some fresh air. I'll be all right. I have some more work to do anyway." Marty was a writer of gay erotica, and he worked from home and often into the night, so it was not unusual for him to suggest Wayne go out on his own.

"You sure?"

"Yeah ... besides you seem a little distracted lately. Why don't you go to The Falcon. I hear the fleet is in town," Marty said with a grin.

Wayne agreed. He stripped off his business clothes, and although it had been a decade, Marty still got a thrill looking at his silver-fur covered muscular lover as he walked to the shower. He thought about joining him but decided it was best to leave Wayne alone.

Within an hour, Wayne was on his way to The Falcon, and Marty was tapping away at his computer.

The Falcon was the town's oldest leather bar, and on some nights, Wayne and Marty could swear there were still patrons there from opening night. However, The Falcon's location was advantageous as it was located near the Norfolk Naval Station, and when the fleet was in, it was hopping with hunky sailors looking for a good time.

Upon Marty's suggestion, Wayne dressed low key this evening and was wearing jeans, a black leather belt, a black T-shirt, and black motorcycle boots. He also decided to go commando, but that didn't stop him from putting on a leather studded cock-ring that Marty had recently bought for him. He entered The Falcon, nodded at a few familiar faces and seated himself at the bar. No sooner had he ordered a beer, when a hunky blond, who was obviously a sailor, sat next to him. Having served in the Navy, Wayne could spot a sailor from a mile away. Marty had also served in the Navy and was still a sailor when he met Wayne.

"What's your rate?" Wayne asked knowing that the word 'rank' did not apply to Navy enlisted men.

"Senior Chief Petty Officer," the blond responded in an equally hunky voice. "You must have served."

"Twenty years ... Master Chief Petty Officer," Wayne responded.

"I guess that makes you the Daddy," the hunk said as he swigged his beer.

Wayne smiled but did not respond.

"So, Master Chief Petty Officer, what are you looking for tonight?"

Wayne took a good long look at the hunk. He was thickly muscled, not unlike Marty, but with piercing blue eyes rather than Marty's green eyes. He had to be no older than thirty.

"What's your name, sailor?"

"Adam, and yours, Daddy?"

"Wayne," he told him while his eyes trailed down to the large basket that strained the crotch of his jeans. Adam was wearing a white T-shirt that hid little of his physique, and Wayne liked what he saw, but again, he just wasn't in the mood. "I have a partner ... we have an understanding ... but I'm just not in the mood to play Daddy tonight ... I hope you understand."

Adam looked right at Wayne, put his hand on Wayne's crotch and said, "Good. Because I'm not in the mood to play boy." He gave Wayne a squeeze, released him and looked up at the TV screen, which was showing some reality nonsense no one cared to watch.

Wayne took a swig of his beer, and suddenly he was intrigued. He had never played submissive. He never had to. His hair had gone prematurely gray, and for as long as he was into the scene, he gladly played the Daddy. Being with Marty was easy because as big as Marty was, he loved being the boy. This was a huge turn-on when they first met as Wayne never dated anyone taller than he, especially someone who was also more muscular, and finding a muscleboy who enjoyed taking orders was a treat indeed. They were also madly in love with each other, but they always had an understanding. They knew men were pigs and monogamy was near impossible. The only rule was they had to give total disclosure – and all the details. Marty loved hearing the details, often including them in his writing or just jacking off while listening to Wayne recount his escapades.

Funny thing was Wayne, who was twenty years older, played way more than Marty did. He once questioned him about this, feeling guilty for always engaging in extracurricular activities. Marty said that as a submissive he oftentimes found it hard to trust people, so he preferred to be careful as the scenes he enjoyed opened someone up to serious injuries if one got carried away. He also assured Wayne that he was totally cool with Wayne playing around, joking that he only had a few good years left. Wayne ended up taking Marty over his knee and spanking him for that comment and ended up with his muscleboy's spunk all over his leg as a result. Then Wayne handcuffed Marty and fucked him doggy-style on the floor as punishment for not feeding his spunk to his Daddy. Marty was sure to let Wayne know when he was about to blow, and Wayne flipped him over and slapped Marty's balls while swallowing his load, and his boy was in heaven.

Wayne looked over at Adam and thought about the proposition. He could not remember the last time someone offered to dominate him. Did anyone ever offer? He thought back but could not recall.

"You got a place?" Wayne asked, surprised at his quickness to respond.

"I got a friend with a basement set-up ... you interested?" Adam said, looking over at Wayne.

Wayne finished his beer, set the bottle on the bar, spun to face Adam and said, "If you got the balls, yeah, I'm interested."

Adam gulped down the rest of his beer, got up from his stool and headed out the bar.

Once outside, he grabbed Wayne's ass and said, "My friend's place is a short drive, you got a car?"

Wayne agreed to drive, and they drove over to Granby Street to his friend's house. Upon pulling into the driveway, Wayne started to get a little nervous. He thought about how Marty said he needed to be careful as a submissive and not all guys could be trusted. Although Adam was a bit shorter than Wayne, he was packed with muscle. Wayne also thought about 'Don't Ask, Don't Tell' and wondered if this guy would kill him when all was said and done to protect his career.

"Listen, I'm not sure ..." Wayne began.

"Hey, I know," Adam interrupted. "Look, I'm not out to hurt you, just have a good time. We'll even set some ground rules if you like."

"OK," Wayne answered. "No bareback, no blood, no scat, and no drugs."

"That's cool. I gotta stay safe if I want to keep my job."

"Nothing that will leave a mark, or at least a permanent one, as I have to go to work on Monday," Wayne said with a smile.

"Totally cool," Adam agreed. He then exited the car, and Wayne did the same.

Wayne stopped Adam before they reached the door, grabbed his arm and said, "And, I don't bottom. I don't get fisted and nothing gets shoved up there."

Adam looked at Wayne's ass and shook his head, "Too bad ... but I guess that's cool, too."

They entered the house, and Adam took off his shirt right after closing the front door. Wayne took a look at Adam's body, and his breath was taken away.

The Senior Chief Petty Officer had the body of a god, covered in light blond hair, and he thought that this guy would be perfect for Marty, who liked that type. He reached over to grab a pec, but Adam grabbed his wrist and said, "I didn't say you could touch me."

"Yes, Sir," Wayne answered as he followed him into the kitchen.

"You want something to drink?"

Thinking he better keep his wits about him, Wayne asked for water. Adam pulled two bottles of water out of the fridge and handed one to Wayne.

"My friend is out to sea, so he said I could use his place whenever I am in town and on leave," he told Wayne.

He then put his bottle down and reached for Wayne's shirt. Wayne didn't resist as Adam pulled his shirt over his head. He obviously liked what he saw and roughly felt Wayne's muscles. He then reached for Wayne's belt, but stopped.

"Take off your boots, boy."

Wayne did as he was ordered.

"Now the jeans."

Wayne again obeyed. He was now naked except for the leather studded cock-ring, and his dick was getting hard and almost to its full thick nine inches. Adam grabbed his dick and said, "Nothing like a boy with a big dick ... you need to piss?"

"Yes, Sir."

"The bathroom's right over there," Adam said as he pointed across the hall. "Leave the door open."

Wayne did as he was told. His dick went down slightly as he started to piss, and just as his stream started, Adam walked in and watched him piss. Wayne looked over, and Adam was now naked with the exception of a brass cock-ring that encased one of the thickest cocks he had ever seen. Wayne figured hard it was probably seven inches and at least seven or even eight around also. Wayne finished pissing and shook his cock, and as he went to step out, Adam stopped him.

"Grab mine, I gotta go."

Wayne wrapped his hand around the Senior Chief Petty Officer's cock and pointed it at the bowl. Adam let go with a strong stream of piss that would make a garden hose jealous, and the feeling of holding that thick rod while it drained caused Wayne's cock to rise up to full attention. When Adam was done, he shook his cock for him, and it started getting hard from the attention.

"Don't move," Adam said as he exited the bathroom.

He returned seconds later with a collar and a leash. He snapped the collar around Wayne's neck and led him out of the bathroom down the hall and downstairs to the basement.

The basement was not the dungeon Wayne expected. There was a bed, a dresser and not much else. It was dimly lit and smelled a bit musty. Adam led Wayne over to the bed and ordered him to lie down on his back. He then took the leash and secured it to the wall on a hook behind the bed. Adam then reached under the bed and grabbed a rubber restraint and secured Wayne's left wrist, walked around and did the same with the right wrist. Adam admired the sight before him then secured Wayne's ankles the same way he secured his wrists.

Wayne was alternating between being turned on and being nervous. Adam sensed this and walked over to the head of the bed, bent down and kissed Wayne hard on the mouth wrestling his tongue with Wayne's.

"Don't worry, boy. Daddy's gonna take good care of you," he said as he released his mouth then he ran his fingers through Wayne's hair.

Wayne's dick started to get hard again as he watched Adam walk over to the dresser and admired how the sailor's muscular butt flexed as he bent down to open the bottom drawer.

Adam turned around holding two nipple clamps and a candle. He walked over to Wayne and scanned his body before putting the nipple clamps on him. Wayne moaned when the clamps were applied, and his cock let out a stream of precum, which did not go unnoticed.

"Whatta ya know, you little pig, leaking like a faucet," Adam said with a smile.

Adam then located a lighter on the dresser and lit the candle. He walked over to Wayne holding the lit candle about twelve inches above Wayne's chest. Wayne felt assured at that moment because an expert knew to hold the candle to allow the wax to cool a bit on its way down and not leave a scar. For the first time, Wayne truly relaxed in Adam's presence.

Wayne flinched when the first drop landed on his chest, and his dick twitched and leaked some more. Adam worked the wax down his torso, and with each drop, Wayne leaked. By the time, Adam reached his balls (he skipped his dick), there was enough precum to fill a bucket. Wayne was in ecstasy as his nipples were pinched hard by the clamps and the hot wax landed on his big smooth balls. He also knew that if Adam kept that up, he was going to come, and somehow Adam also sensed this. He stopped dripping wax on Wayne and blew out the candle.

Adam walked back over to the bed and twisted one of the nipple clamps causing Wayne to half moan, half scream, then he squeezed the other one getting the same reaction. Without saying a word, Adam climbed on top of Wayne and straddled his face, facing away from him, dropping his huge nuts toward his mouth and his ass toward his nose.

"Lick my balls, boy."

Wayne went to town on those furry balls. He slathered them and rolled them in his mouth and tried to get both in his mouth at once. This was not easy considering he was restrained and collared. Adam's muscular legs did a good job of holding him up, so he did not crush Wayne's face, but this was not easy as Wayne was an oral expert, and Adam's cock was leaking almost as much as Wayne's. Adam then scooted forward.

"Lick my hot hole, boy."

And, Wayne did as he was told. He did his best to get his tongue between those muscular cheeks and licked the blond fur-covered hole, almost coming just from the feeling of having this musclehunk squatting over his face.

Adam never experienced anything like Wayne's technique, and the sight of Wayne's huge leaking cock was making him want more. He let Wayne get him really wet then he hopped off the bed.

"Good boy."

Wayne's tongue was sore, but in a good way.

Adam walked over to the dresser again and opened the top drawer and pulled out a bottle of Gun Oil, a packet of condoms and a ball gag.

Wayne started to protest, but Adam was quick to place the ball gag over his mouth. Now, Wayne was starting to get scared again, but Adam leaned down, ran his fingers through his hair and said, "Relax, boy. I know the rules." Then he grabbed Wayne's still raging dick. "And you better not lose this hard-on, boy."

Adam opened the condom packet with his teeth and rolled it onto Wayne's dick. He then pumped some of the Gun Oil into his palm, rubbed some on Wayne's cock and then lubed his ass with his own fingers.

"Now, boy, if you fuck Daddy really good, I'll have a nice treat for you."

Adam again straddled Wayne, but facing him this time, and with one fell swoop impaled himself on Wayne's thick nine inches. He then grabbed the nipple clamps and rode that hard cock while twisting on those clamps. Wayne bucked up as best he could while the blond musclehunk sailor gave his own quads a good workout riding him up and down. Adam's thick cock grew even thicker with each thrust, and the head was swollen and purple and smacking against his belly. Wayne felt his own cock growing in length as he felt sensations he had not felt in a long time.

"Come on, boy, fuck me good!" Adam ordered.

With the ball gag, he was finding it hard to respond, but his eyes said it all.

Adam stopped twisting the clamps and flexed his biceps for Wayne and licked them admiring himself in the process while continuing to squat up and down on the large cock that impaled his hot hole. He then ran his hands over his pecs and gave Wayne quite a muscle show, flexing and feeling and licking himself.

'How does he know how much flexing turns me on?' Wayne thought. 'If he doesn't stop, I'm going to shoot!'

Adam continued to flex and squat until his dick was so hard it hurt. He reached down while still riding Wayne and removed the ball gag. Then, he pulled off Wayne's dick, moved forward and shoved his aching cock into Wayne's mouth, and his extra-thick cock shot a huge load into his mouth and down his throat. Wayne swallowed every delicious drop. All this action was too much for him, and he shot a huge load of his own into the condom that was still on his dick.

Adam stepped off the bed and looked down at the cum-filled rubber, and out of breath, but laughing, he said, "You fucking cum pig."

Wayne said nothing as he tried to catch his breath and continued to taste the semen from the sailor.

Adam then undid the restraints and the collar, and Wayne thanked him.

"You may wanna shower before you go home," Adam said.

Wayne took him up on his offer and once cleaned up and dressed was ready to leave, totally satisfied.

"Thank you, Sir. That was just what I needed," Wayne said as he shook Adam's hand.

"Well, it is what Marty said you wanted," Adam said with a wink.

"That little shit," Wayne responded shaking his head.

"Hey he ain't so little, and be nice to him. There aren't too many partners who would do what he did for you," Adam admonished.

Wayne knew Adam was right and knew at that moment he loved Marty more than anything.

"Tell me then. Did you ever bottom for Marty?" Wayne asked.

"With a cock like his? Of course. Don't you?" Adam asked as if the answer were obvious.

Wayne didn't answer. He gave Adam his number and suggested a three-way sometime, which Adam eagerly agreed would be fun.

Wayne arrived home an hour later to find Marty had already gone to bed. He stripped off his clothes and crawled into bed with his lover. Marty moaned as Wayne spooned him and grabbed his Daddy's hand, pulling it to his chest.

"Did you have a good time, Daddy?" he asked sleepily.

"If you fuck me, boy, I'll tell you all about it," Wayne growled.

Marty's eyes popped open, for he wasn't sure he heard what he thought he heard.

Wayne then pulled Marty on top of him, wrapped his legs around his boy's waist and begged him to drive his huge cock into him. Marty immediately grabbed some lube from the nightstand, greased up Wayne's asshole and rammed his huge hard cock all the way into his Daddy before he changed his mind.

In ten years, he had never fucked Wayne, and he was not about to miss this opportunity. Wayne didn't protest Marty's rough treatment and no-holds-barred fucking, actually getting totally turned on and rock-hard from the way his boy wasted no time impaling him. Marty leaned in and kissed him roughly and told him how much he loved him, while Wayne reciprocated, and Marty gave his Daddy the ride of a lifetime, practically fucking him into the next building. Wayne loved every minute of it as his muscleboy pounded his virgin hole with all his super strength, feeling those huge balls slap against his ass while Marty's muscular body glistened with sweat from the workout.

It was a total muscle fuck.

And, all the neighbors heard for hours that night was "Fuck me, boy! Come on, you can fuck Daddy harder than that!" along with the grunts and heavy breathing of a muscleboy giving his Daddy the ride of a lifetime.

Anchors aweigh!

LASSO AND TLEM

The day was getting late, but according to the old man at the ranch, the next real town in the Arizona Territory was only a dozen or so miles away. He hoped to find a blacksmith when he arrived as Montgomery, his horse, needed new shoes.

The sun was blazing, more than Lasso ever experienced being raised in Virginia. Sure, the summers were hot, but nothing like this. Lasso didn't know much about temperatures, but he guessed this to be hot enough to cook beans without a fire. He stopped at a pond, one of just a few he had encountered over the last few days, and he hopped off Montgomery, so the poor horse could get a drink and some rest.

Lasso stretched and decided he better fill his canteen and get a drink himself. He leaned over to the pond and filled his canteen then scooped a few swallows of water into his palm to quench his parched throat. He checked out his reflection in the water.

Saying that Lasso was narcissistic would be an understatement. He was damn good-looking, and he knew it, and if you didn't think he was good-looking, just ask him. He was six-foot-six and weighed in at over 240 pounds. His black, wavy hair was shaggy but fell perfectly over his square face with his dark eye brows, deep black eyes, strong jaw and rare for anyone at that time, perfectly straight teeth framed by full lips.

Lasso reached up and patted Montgomery, the only thing he loved more than himself, and his horse neighed appreciatively.

"I'll walk you the rest of the way, old girl."

Lasso stood up, placed his canteen back in the bag hanging behind his saddle, and grabbed Montgomery's reins.

He walked a few miles before stopping to strip off his shirt, revealing his hairy muscular physique, built from years of ranch work and roping cattle.

After about an hour, Lasso spotted what looked to be the beginnings of a town, if one could call it that – just a strip of buildings on a dirt road, maybe ten if that many. He stopped and put his shirt back on before going any further as he didn't want to draw too much attention to himself being so good-looking and all.

As he approached the outskirts of this town, he saw a sign that said, "Welcome to Nemtoh, Arizona, Population 69."

"I guess this is it, Montgomery. Now let's see about getting you some new shoes."

Montgomery answered with an affirmative neigh.

As he walked down the main street – the only street – in Nemtoh, Lasso noticed only a few people, all men actually, walking around. And, all of them, though handsome, every one of them, looked at him with suspicion. He spotted a young blond guy, tall, strapping and looking especially clean for someone in a town like this.

"Excuse me, mister," Lasso called out.

"Yes," the blond answered as he pushed up his hat.

"Is there a blacksmith in this town?"

"What's your name?" the blond asked.

"Name's Lasso, is there a blacksmith?"

"What brings you to Nemtoh?" the blond asked without answering the initial question, and this was beginning to piss Lasso off.

"Look, I'm not here to start trouble. I'm on my way to work at a ranch fifty miles west of here, and my horse needs new shoes."

"What ranch?" the blond asked insistently.

"Jeez, man, what's your problem? Is this some kind of private community? Fuck it! I'll just let my horse suffer until I find the next town." And, Lasso turned his horse around and started to walk back to the main trail.

"Wait a minute, Lasso," the blond called out. "It's just that we're a quiet town, and we like to know who's coming through."

Lasso stopped and turned around. He hesitated before speaking, "So, what are you? The goddamn marshal or something?"

"Actually, I'm the mayor, Mayor Bottumzup."

Lasso smiled and stifled a giggle, "Did you say bottom's up?"

"Bottumzup, and I've heard them all. I don't want to see your horse suffer ... the blacksmith is over there," Bottumzup said, pointing to a building across the street. "His name is Tlem."

"Tlem? Thanks," Lasso said as he walked Montgomery over to where the mayor pointed.

"If you need to stay the night, we have a hotel over there," the mayor said pointing to another building with a sign out front that read, "Hothole Hotel – No Women Allowed."

"Thanks," Lasso answered as he continued toward the blacksmith's building then stopped to read the hotel sign again to be sure he saw what he thought he saw. He did. He pushed his cowboy hat up and shook his head, wondering what kind of town he had stumbled upon.

Lasso entered the blacksmith's building slowly and looked around before spotting a very tall, muscular black man, wearing no shirt, a leather apron and those new-fangled dungarees or blue jeans as they called them in California.

"Are you Tlem?" Lasso called out.

The man turned around, and Lasso got a good look at his face, which was very handsome, with a strong jaw and equally full lips like Lasso's, but the blacksmith's muscular torso was devoid of hair, although glistening with sweat, and Lasso felt a stream of precum drip out of his cock and down his left leg.

"Name's Lasso," he said as he reached out to shake the man's hand, "Montgomery here needs a new set of shoes. How long will that take?"

The blacksmith shook Lasso's hand and spoke for the first time, "Kinda backed up, I can have her ready by tomorrow morning."

Lasso pulled out his watch. It was getting pretty late, and he wasn't about to make it to his new job before tomorrow anyway. "Sounds good. I guess I'll stay at that hotel tonight. Should I pay you now or tomorrow?"

"I like to be paid when I'm done," Tlem said then he took Montgomery's reigns and led her to a stall where he had water and hay ready for her to enjoy. "See you in the morning, Lasso."

Lasso took one more long look at the blacksmith before heading over to the Hothole Hotel to make sure the sight was etched into his memory.

For a very small town, the Hothole was quite a fancy hotel. But, Lasso figured that they were the only place to stay in these parts as the railroad hadn't even made it this far. The manager was another handsome Nemtoh citizen, albeit a bit older than the others he saw outside. There were a few patrons at the bar, all looking a little too clean for life in the Arizona Territory, but Lasso didn't mind as he had seen enough filthy men since heading west a few months ago.

"How many nights will you be staying, Mr. Lasso?"

"Just the one. Gotta head out to a job on a ranch tomorrow," Lasso answered.

"Very good, sir. That will be three dollars."

Lasso handed three silver dollars to the manager thinking the price a bit steep, but didn't complain.

"Would you be needing a bath? We can launder your clothes also."

Lasso was puzzled, bath, laundry, who heard of such a thing out here? He pretty much gave up on bathtubs since leaving Virginia using ponds and streams to wash up and launder his clothes. "Yeah, that would be good. Pretty clean town you have here."

"Well, Mr. Lasso, just because this is a small town in the Arizona Territory doesn't mean we have to live like Barbarians," the manager said with a wink.

The manager handed Lasso his room key and told him someone would be up to take him to the washroom within the hour.

Lasso didn't realize how tired he was. No sooner had he entered the room, stripped off all his clothes and climbed onto the bed that he closed his eyes and fell asleep.

He was awakened by the sound of someone in his room. As he opened his eyes, he saw what looked to be a young man, who seemed to be a hotel employee.

"I didn't mean to wake you, sir. I was just returning your laundry."

"How long was I asleep?"

"About three hours, sir. You may take your bath now. The washroom is down the hall on the right, and I have filled your tub with hot water. Here is a towel for you," and the young man handed him the softest towel he ever felt.

Lasso climbed out of the bed and wrapped the towel around him, noticing the young man stealing a peek. He exited the room and walked down the hall and located a room marked 'Wash Room.' He opened the door, and there were two tubs in the room, which was decorated as nicely as the lobby, with a wood stove for heating water and nice curtains over the windows. One tub was occupied, so Lasso closed the door behind him and walked toward the empty tub. As he looked over at the other tub, he saw that Tlem was relaxing in the sudsy water.

Tlem opened his eyes and saw Lasso standing there wearing nothing but a towel.

"You finished with Montgomery already?" Lasso asked.

"Yep, that'll be three dollars."

"No pockets here, I'll pay you after my bath," Lasso told him as he looked over the blacksmith's upper torso and felt his cock start to swell.

"So why do they call you Lasso?" Tlem asked, looking at Lasso as if he were a meal for the tasting.

Lasso removed his towel revealing his slightly swelling uncut cock, whose foreskin barely concealed the large head, which was already reaching nine inches and still had at least two to go. "That's why."

Tlem licked his lips and said, "Impressive."

Lasso climbed into the tub hoping the water would calm him down. "Why do they call you Tlem?"

Tlem looked over at Lasso, then he stood up and revealed a hefty cock that matched Lasso's in length and girth, but was getting harder by the second. Lasso looked at the muscular blacksmith with his large, hard black cock pointing at him and tried to act nonchalant, although he had been hungry for a big piece of meat for days.

"Beautiful, but what does Tlem have to do with that?"

"Three-legged man was my nickname on the plantation. When they granted me my freedom, I chose the name Tlem."

The blacksmith then walked over to Lasso's tub and leaned down next to him, looking him right in the eyes. Without saying another word, he placed his calloused hand behind Lasso's head and pulled him in for a long hard kiss, and Lasso thought he would shoot his load right there as his big dick reached its full eleven inches in seconds.

With his other hand, Tlem reached into the tub and grabbed the hard member and started to stroke it without losing his mouth's grip on Lasso's. The ranch-hand reached under Tlem and grabbed his hard eleven inches and matched him stroke for stroke. They kept this up for quite a while without releasing their mouths, moaning and breathing hard, and slurping ...

"I'm gonna blow, if you keep that up," Tlem said, finally releasing Lasso's mouth.

"Me, too," Lasso answered.

With that, Tlem stood up walked around, so he was behind Lasso's head and leaned down so his cock aimed at the ranch-hand's mouth and continued leaning over until Lasso's cock was aiming for his. Both men needed no instruction as they each began to feast on the other's enormous meat, and it was not long before they both fed each other huge loads of ranch-hand and blacksmith cum.

Finally, releasing Lasso's cock, Tlem said, "For that, I'll give you a discount on the shoes."

"That was all I had to do for a discount?" Lasso asked smiling and looking up at this beautiful blacksmith.

"I'll let you have them for free if you do me one other favor."

"What's that?" Lasso asked.

"My horse, York, needs some release, too, and he kinda took a liking to Montgomery. Let him have his fun ..."

"Wait, I can't have a pregnant horse while working on the ranch ..." Lasso protested.

"Let me finish," Tlem interrupted. "I own a ranch just outside of town. You come work for me, and I'll pay you whatever you were supposed to get where you're going."

"Why should I do that?" Lasso asked.

"Because nowhere else in the Arizona territory are you gonna find a town full of men who like doing what we just did, and you can live in my house and do it with me all the time," Tlem said with a wink.

Lasso didn't need any more persuasion and agreed to Tlem's terms, and both he and Montgomery ended up happy in their new home ...

... and if this were a movie, the next scene would have them riding off into the sunset – naked.

THE AFTER-WORKOUT

Bobby always worked out at 5:00 am, walking from his home in Columbia Heights in Washington, DC, down 16th Street, to Results the Gym on U Street, in the dark, early morning hours six days a week. His friends worried that he would get mugged one day, but Bobby wasn't worried. Even though he was only five-foot-five, he weighed in at almost 170 pounds, and all of that was solid muscle. Some joked that at least twenty of it was cock as Bobby was known for his endowment, which would make a horse envious. This was another reason he chose to work out so early. Results had open showers, and Bobby grew tired of all the stares he would get while showering since his dick hung at least to mid-thigh even under the coldest spray. When he was done working out around 6:00 am, he was usually the only one in the shower, which suited him just fine.

This particular morning, Bobby was shampooing his hair after a grueling chest workout when he heard a showerhead being turned on, then another. Great, he thought to himself, more gawkers. Bobby turned around, so his back was to the wall as he rinsed the shampoo from his hair, and when he opened his eyes, he almost gasped at what he saw. He blinked twice to be sure he was not hallucinating. Standing across from him, using adjacent showers were identical twins, and these were no ordinary twins. They were blond, blue-eyed Adonises, over six-feet tall, with god-like physiques and hanging between their legs were the largest dicks Bobby had ever seen soft, with the exception of his own of course.

The twins pretty much ignored Bobby as they soaped up and rinsed off. Bobby decided to do the same, but he had to face the wall, for staring at the twins would surely cause his cock to swell, and there would be no hiding *his* hard-on. The three men finished showering at the same time, dried off and made their way to their lockers to get dressed. Bobby finished dressing first, and after deciding against introducing himself, he left the gym and proceeded to walk back home up 16th Street.

As he crossed Florida Avenue, Bobby noticed a car across the street that was moving in the same direction he was but rather slowly. He thought nothing of it, figuring it was probably one of the newspaper delivery drivers making his early rounds.

He walked just a few yards more when the car sped up, then made a sudden tire-squealing U-turn and stopped in front of Bobby. Before he could react, the passenger side door opened, and a man grabbed Bobby, placed a hand with a handkerchief over his mouth and threw him into the back seat of the car. Then, the car sped off.

Bobby blinked open his eyes and did not know where he was or how long he had been there. He tried to say something, but he had a ball gag in his mouth, and when he looked down, he saw that he was naked and strapped to a table on his back. He looked around the room and noticed it was a basement with little to no furniture that he could see from his vantage point. He started to panic and hyperventilate just as one of his captors entered the room.

It was one of the twins from the gym, and he was now standing over Bobby wearing nothing but a pair of lederhosen. The Adonis noticed Bobby was hyperventilating, so he removed the ball gag and put a paper bag over Bobby's mouth. Bobby breathed into the bag, and his captor kept the bag there until his breathing calmed down.

Once the bag was removed, Bobby started shouting, "Where am I? Who are you? What are you doing with me?"

The twin said nothing. He placed a finger over his mouth to indicate that Bobby should stop shouting. Bobby calmed down and waited for the blond to say something. But, nothing was said. Then, the other twin entered the room, dressed in identical lederhosen and stood on the other side of Bobby. The twins looked at each other then the twin to his right spoke.

"If you promise not to shout, we will make this as pleasant as possible, but if you do shout, you will regret the day you were born."

Quietly, Bobby asked, "Make what pleasant?"

"This experience, of course," the other twin said. "We just want to have a little fun with you, and if we enjoy ourselves, we will let you go when we are done, but if we find you tedious, we will torture you until you beg for your own death."

Bobby didn't have to think long about his options. He was apparently strapped tightly to the table, and even if he did manage to get loose, these guys were twice his size.

They looked at Bobby and smiled, then opened their lederhosen, pulled out their enormous dicks and proceeded to piss all over Bobby. The little muscleman was no stranger to water sports, so this did not bother him as long as they avoided his face, and fortunately they did even though they seemed to piss a gallon each. The stench of their urine permeated the room, and Bobby could only wonder what was yet to come as he had never before been in a situation such as this. Once their bladders were empty, they removed their lederhosen and ran their hands all over Bobby's thickly muscled body working the piss into every pore.

One grabbed his balls and gave them a good yank, causing Bobby to grunt, while the other squeezed his dick, which was now starting to fill even though he tried to keep it from getting hard. But, it was to no avail, as the hands torturing his cock and balls were doing more to turn him on than frighten him, and within a minute, his dick was at its full ten inches, which on his five-foot-five frame brought the mushroom head to right below his pecs.

The twin to his right hit a button under the table, and suddenly Bobby's legs were being pulled up and apart by some sort of pulley device he had not noticed before, and the contraption did not stop until Bobby was suspended by his ankles with only his shoulders on the table. Then the twin to his left hit a button, and the same thing happened to his wrists until he was suspended by his wrists and ankles, spreadeagled from both ends with no support for his back. He thought he was going to be quartered, when the twin to his right reached up and pulled down a leather strap, passed it under his back to the other twin, who then connected it to a hook in the ceiling, thus supporting Bobby's back. The table was then rolled away, and Bobby was lowered until he was just below waist level of his captors.

The twin on his right then moved down to his feet and positioned himself between his legs while the other one went to the other side of the room to get a cart and wheel it over to where his brother was standing. In spite of all this, Bobby's dick refused to go down. He wondered if he was suffering from Stockholm Syndrome. *But, doesn't that take a few months or even years?* He thought.

Bobby could not see what was on the table but guessed at least one of the items was grease or lard, as he felt his ass being slathered with something thick and gloppy. Then he felt the intruder – one, maybe two, maybe even three fingers being forced into his ass, twisting and probing with no finesse at all. Bobby gritted his teeth and took the intrusion like a man as the other twin walked over to his left and stood by his head.

Bobby looked over and saw that he now sported a huge hard-on that rivaled his in size, and it was sticking straight out at his face with precum practically pouring from the slit. Bobby involuntarily licked his lips, and this captor shoved his enormous meat into Bobby's mouth without ceremony. Bobby figured if they were going to kill him, he might as well go out with a smile, so he sucked hungrily on the huge cock in his mouth, which continued to leak pints of precum that tasted better than he would acknowledge to these two bastards.

As he was chowing down on the manmeat, he felt the fingers exit his asshole, only to be rudely replaced by the other huge cock in the room, all greased up and practically up to his nipples within seconds. Then the pounding began – from both ends.

The twins showed no mercy as they used the little muscle man for their own pleasure as if he were just a hole to be plugged and filled with cock. No attention was given to Bobby's dick, which now ached it was so hard, while his huge balls drew up, ready to explode.

The twins had great staying power and pumped and pumped for quite a while, or at least it seemed quite a while, until the one in Bobby's mouth exploded with a yell, and shot pint after pint of his thick cum down Bobby's throat, which he didn't lose a drop of. Then, his brother yelled identically and left his own quart of milk in Bobby's ass, causing Bobby to shoot a load to be envied all over his torso with a few shots hitting his chin.

The twins exited their respective holes, and Bobby thought, *That's it?* And, with that, a hand with a handkerchief was placed over his face again.

Bobby opened his eyes, and after looking up, saw that a couple of people were staring down at him, including a police officer. He shook his head, and after looking around, realized he was in Meridian Hill Park.

The police officer helped him up and asked, "Are you OK? How long have you been lying there?"

"What time is it?" Bobby asked.

"Around 8:00 am," the officer answered, and Bobby took a good look at him. He was over six feet tall, blond and obviously built and hung. He then looked out to 16th Street at the patrol car and saw an identical officer waiting for his partner.

"Only two hours?" Bobby asked. "That's the best you could do?"

And, Bobby stood up and walked away with a smile.

GAYDAR

Every morning, he jogs past me as I walk my dog. Then on the way back, he jogs by again and says hello. And, this happens every morning at 4:30 am.

I wonder about him, this man who jogs that early in the morning. I have been getting up that early for years to walk my dog then go to the gym. For months, he has jogged past me then back again in the other direction.

I want to say more, ask him his name, see what he is about, but who stops a jogger to have a conversation?

Then it stops.

I don't see him jogging at that early hour anymore.

I also walk my dog after the gym around 6:30 am. And, one morning he jogs past me? Does he jog twice, or have his hours changed?

Why am I so obsessed with him? Why do I care?

It is over 90 degrees, why doesn't he take his shirt off?

He always wears the same thing, blue shorts and yellow muscle shirt. It isn't even a tank top.

He doesn't have an iPod, so saying hello is no problem.

Where does his run stop, so I can approach him?

I need to get over myself.

I think of ways to get his attention. I have a wife-beater on under my T-shirt, and I am all pumped from the gym. It is hotter than blazes and humid, too, even at this early hour, so I take off my shirt as if I am just a little too hot.

There I am, walking my dog in nothing but a wife beater, all pumped and sweaty. This will get his attention.

He jogs past me again in the other direction – so predictable. He stares at me and checks out my body for more than a few seconds, then says something like have a good morning, or good morning, or nice seeing you this morning. And, he is up the street before I can respond.

He *is* gay. No straight guy checks a guy out like that. He was eyeing me from head to toe.

The next morning, he jogs by again. I walk my dog in nothing but the wife-beater, and I decide to take it off. Now I am pumped and shirtless, and just as always, he jogs by me again in the other direction.

But, this time he doesn't look, and when I say good morning, he mumbles.

That is what I get for being obvious. I immediately put the wife-beater back on.

Now, I have made a fool of myself, and I obsess about it all day.

I never see him again – not at 4:30 am, not at 6:30 am.

I guess that is the end of that.

A few weeks later, I am walking my dog at night. I see him walking toward me with a woman. The closer he gets, I notice the woman is pregnant, quite pregnant.

He says hello and introduces his wife and tells me he stopped jogging due to a knee injury.

I forget his name.

What does it matter? He's straight, married and expecting a baby.

My gaydar is all fucked up.

But, I'll go to my grave swearing he cruised me that one morning.

THE WINDOW ESTIMATE

I hate being an apartment manager, and I only agreed to do it because my landlords promised me a fifty percent reduction in the rent for the four years they would be in Brazil. The worst part is that I have to listen to the constant complaining from the fat redneck, her drunk asshole of a husband and her future serial killer, slut daughter upstairs. I just wish the daughter would get it over with and kill them already, so I can clean up the mess and rent the place out to a couple of hotties. But, until then, I have to be the responsible one and that includes getting estimates for work that I would rather let go in the hopes the cast from *Cops* upstairs will leave in frustration.

Most of the time, these estimates are for things they have broken, and I know that the constant yelling and banging that goes on is the reason the frame of the large bay window in their master bedroom was cracked causing the glass to fall down into the wall, leaving a four-inch gap on the top.

I took my sweet time getting an estimate, but when the rain seeped in causing water to leak into my apartment, it became my personal problem, so I called a couple of window companies. I figured I would punish the landlords as well for sticking me with these assholes and get an estimate for all the windows.

Two salesmen had been here already, but they were so slick, I threw away their estimates before the door closed behind them.

On the day the third and final guy was to arrive, I pretty much didn't care anymore. I decided to work from home that day, so it was amazing I even bothered to shower, although I only wore a pair of gym shorts (actually cut-off sweat pants) and a wife-beater. I was totally engrossed in work when I heard a knock at the door.

I opened the door and standing there was what looked to be a teenager, wearing a loose fitting All-Weather Window Company polo shirt. He gave me the taillights to headlights three-second once over I tend to get from guys who see me for the first time, which doesn't even faze me anymore.

You see, I am an ex-professional football player (not that anyone remembers – third string center), and I am six-foot even, weighing in at around two-hundred-sixty pounds. At thirty-five, I still work out as if I am being paid to, and I won't deny I ever took a needle in the ass. We'll leave it at that. Now, I work as a bookkeeper for a nondescript company in a nondescript cubicle located in a nondescript building. I am one of the lucky few to have actually gotten paid to be a professional football player, but after almost five years on the bench, I got bored. I was told I was too nice, not aggressive enough, but the coach liked me, so I held onto my job.

Now, the kid in front of me may have played some sports. He had that college jock, too many frat parties body. You know the type – broad shoulders, decent arms, and remnants of the 'freshman forty' still around the middle. If they are straight, the paunch is there for life, and if they are gay, well, they wouldn't have taken on the freshman-forty in the first place. No gay boy in his twenties would allow such a thing to happen to him. This kid was definitely straight, which was fine with me as I don't like them young. I like them older, much older. I like being fucked silly by a big musclebear with gray hair. If this kid had a twelve-inch dick, I couldn't have cared less.

"Mr. Kennedy?"

I let him in, and he introduced himself as Allan. I showed him all the windows upstairs and downstairs in all the apartments. Of course, the redneck had to butt in and say what she wanted in a window, but I shut her up immediately and continued to follow Allan from wall to wall while he measured and wrote on his legal pad.

When we were done, we returned to my apartment, and I had to ask him his age.

"I'm twenty-three. I couldn't find a job in my field, so I took this sales job, which has made my college education a waste ... can I ask you a question, a personal question?"

I said sure.

"I can see you work out ..."

He could see I work out. He was brilliant. My arms relaxed are eighteen inches around. My pecs are so huge, I can't see my feet, and he can see I work out.

"I've been trying to lose this gut since I graduated, and nothing I do works. Should I do more cardio?"

"You should quit drinking so much beer," I said and raised my eyebrows. I may let a quack doc shoot what is probably horse piss into my ass to get huge and ripped, but I never drank or did drugs. Yeah, I know, what I do is just as bad. Whatever. You'd fuck me if you had a chance, especially if you saw my rock hard and huge bubble-butt.

"Yeah, I guess you're right."

"So, how long before I get an estimate?" I asked.

"Oh, I can have one for you this afternoon. I'll email it to you."

And with that, he was gone.

I went back to work and took a mid-day break to go to the gym because I have body dysmorphia or manorexia or some other psychological shit because I think I'm fat or skinny and have deep emotional issues. Please. I know what I look like. I look like a fucking freak, but I like the freak look, and the old musclebear dads I let fuck me like it, too. Don't assume you know guys like me.

After I returned from the gym, I was mixing myself a protein shake when there was a knock at the door. I was back in my cut-off sweat shorts but not wearing a shirt anymore. I opened the door, and it was frat-boy window guy.

"I decided to hand deliver the estimate," he said as he handed me the envelope. "I can explain it to you if you like?"

I gave him my best you think I am a dunder-headed muscleboy with the IQ of a baboon look.

"Oh, I didn't mean it like that ... uh, I mean I like to explain why we may be higher than most anyone else," Allan recovered.

"I may look mean, but it takes a whole hell of a lot to offend me or piss me off ... believe me, kid, I haven't lost my temper in years," I said with a smile as I motioned him inside.

What, you say? A juiced-up freak who hasn't had a roid induced hissy fit? See, you read too much. I have never been a hot head. That is why I sucked as a professional football player. I'm too easy going. The only side effect I ever got from the juice was shrunken balls, but I can still come a gallon of spunk.

I offered Allan a protein shake, and he accepted. As we sat there drinking our whey concoctions, he explained all the window crap, and I pretended to listen, but I couldn't get over how he was avoiding looking at me. I was shirtless, pumped from the gym and sitting no more than two feet away from him. Although I had showered at the gym, I hadn't bothered putting on deodorant, so I had a light musk about me, which some guys like.

When he finally looked up, I could tell he was enthralled by my pumped pecs and my nipples, which I pulled on constantly. They stick out a good inch even now.

"You want to touch them?" I asked.

His eyes bulged.

"Look, it won't make you gay. Straight guys always want to touch my muscles to see what they feel like. Are they hard, soft, will they vibrate?" I said with a chuckle and a smile.

"Sure," he said as he slowly reached over to kind of poke a finger at my bicep.

I flexed it for him, and he then caressed it a bit before taking his hand away. So, I was wrong about him. He was a big ole fag. I grabbed his hand and put it on my pec while I made it bounce.

"Damn, they are hard as a rock," he said.

I was not turned on by this. He just wasn't my type. Yeah, I know, get over it.

"Now, about this estimate. What can we do to get you to come down by at least ten percent?" I may have been pissed at the landlords, but I was still a tightwad at heart, and I wasn't going for the obvious scene you are expecting here.

"Become my personal trainer," he said.

I sat back and looked at him. He had potential and a good frame. And that gut he complained about wasn't really that bad, just a little soft.

"Take off your shirt," I said.

He stood up and without hesitation removed his shirt. His shoulders were broad, and his biceps a nice size, too. However, his chest was a surprise as it was huge, which made me make a mental note to suggest he wear a tighter company shirt, and it was covered with hair, curly blond hair that trailed down to his pants.

"You'll have to shave that," I said pointing to his chest.

"Really?" he said as he ran his hand seductively down his torso.

"But not until after you bend me over this table and fuck my brains out. The condoms and lube are in the drawer behind you. If you want me to train you, you better be ready to do what I say at the drop of a hat," I said without stopping to take a breath. Then I stood, dropped my cut-off sweat shorts revealing my hard five-inch dick. Yeah, I know, everyone in these stories is hung like a horse. Well, I'm a bottom, and I may not have a lot of dick to play with, but I certainly have enough muscle to make up for it. Besides, little dicks get hard, stay hard, and shoot nice creamy loads. So, get over it.

I also know that I said he wasn't my type. But, I wanted that estimate lowered, and my hole filled at the same time. He was there; I was horny; do the math.

I then bent over the table, while he fumbled around with his pants.

"Hurry up, I don't get this horny often, just grease it up and plug me," I said over my shoulder.

I then felt the cold lube dribbling down my crack. He sort of rubbed it all around, and I could tell he was nervous. I then heard the condom wrapper being opened; he cursed himself while he tried to roll it on. I clearly had him flustered.

"Are these the largest ones you have?" he asked.

I turned around and saw what looked to be a good ten thick inches of circumcised dick sticking straight out at me. There you go – a horse-hung top in a porno story. Are you happy now?

"Look in the back of the drawer. They must have slid back. There should be some extra-hungs or whatever they call them," I said as I marveled at his heat-seeking moisture missile, which is a friend's nickname for huge cocks.

"Found them," he said with delight.

"Good, slip one on and fuck my brains out," I said as I again bent over the table. "And, don't bother eating me out or fingering me, just stick that barbell up my chute ... I hate foreplay."

He did just that. All the way in, no apologies, no hesitation, no finesse, no bullshit, and I loved it.

"Now, reach around and pull my nipples as hard as you can while you fuck me."

And, he did just that. He reached around and pulled my big nipples, no apologies, no hesitation, no finesse, no bullshit, and I loved it.

He practically pounded my huge muscular ass over the moon (excuse the pun) and pulled my nipples another inch. I was in heaven. He was having a pretty good time, too. Or, he was good at faking it because he kept telling me what a hot ass I had and what a sexy motherfucker I was. And at one point, he started nibbling on the back of my neck, and that did it.

I cried out as I came. I wasn't even touching myself since I was using my hands to hold onto the edge of the table while he pounded me for points. And, right after I came, he filled that extra large rubber with his own load and yelled out loud what a "man slut" I was, and amazingly, I came again – hands free.

When he recovered, he apologized for calling me a man slut and gave me ten percent off on the windows in addition to another ten percent for the hot fuck.

I never told him, but calling me a man slut was the best part of the fuck.

The windows look great. And Allan? He is a muscle freak now, too.

I love being me.

THE CENTER OF ATTENTION

Billy played center for as long as he played football, beginning with peewee, then middle school, high school, and now college. For some reason, coaches automatically put him in that position, bent over with a quarterback's hands up his crotch. Was it his size? He was always the tallest – and widest – kid with the ability to run over anyone headed for the quarterback like a steam roller? Or, was it his round muscular butt, which was so tantalizing in that position. He never thought it was his butt. After all, he had a talent for hiking the ball and immediately knocking down at least three defensive linemen before they knew what hit them. Years of playing football in his hometown of Newport News gave him a reputation, and many a lineman would try to challenge Billy, but by the end of the game, the quarterback on Billy's team would never have a scratch on him.

He entered college with a full scholarship. By eighteen, his frame had filled out quite nicely, and now in his senior year at age twenty-one, he was, as one of the cheerleaders called him, 'hunkalicious.' Billy was over six-foot-five, weighing more than 280 pounds, with a chest that measured at least fifty-four inches, biceps that approached twenty inches, a waist that although thirty-eight inches was tight and ripped, quads that measured over thirty-five inches and of course, that big round muscular butt. While many of his teammates were using steroids and other 'enhancements,' Billy had no desire to do anything that wasn't natural. He didn't have to as he was one of the lucky few who could get more muscular just from looking at a dumbbell. To make his teammates more jealous, Billy had inherited the best of both his Russian and Moroccan genes – smooth dark skin, strong facial features, green eyes, thick curly hair and bright white teeth. His hands and feet were huge, and he could palm a football with no problem.

Their first two seasons were highly successful with few losses, so the team was quite surprised when their coach resigned under pressure, and a new coach from a Southern university was brought in. And along with that new coach arrived a new quarterback. The new quarterback was not unexpected as Jerry Garrison had graduated the prior year and was playing pro-ball now. Billy wasn't envious, for he was not looking forward to a pro football career. He was a straight-A pre-med student, and he was actually looking forward to ending his football days. After all, he had been playing center since he was six years old, and all the practices were getting old.

The team entered the locker room silently the day after the announcement of their new coach and quarterback. As they changed into their practice uniforms, there was grumbling about the new coach's reputation, rumors and gossip that Billy didn't care to hear. The advantage to playing center was that all he had to do was remember when to hike the ball, plow forward and hope he hadn't hurt a defensive lineman – too badly.

After changing, they ran out to the field and lined up, awaiting the introductions.

Billy looked to his right and spotted a tall, black man with an almost equally tall, but younger, black man beside him. The older man looked to be in his mid-thirties, around six-foot-three and muscular. Billy guessed he played football in his youth and maintained his athletic physique. He was wearing a tight white polo shirt that accentuated his large chest and bulging biceps and blue coaching shorts that did little to hide his full basket. He was wearing a cap, but Billy could tell the man had a shaved head, and the hat did not hide the fact that he was perhaps the most handsome man he had ever seen with dark smooth skin and a bright smile surrounded by thick sexy lips. The younger of the two looked to be about Billy's age and maybe only an inch shorter if that much. He was muscular but leaner than the older man. His hair was cut short, and he had high cheek bones, a wide sexy mouth and big dark eyes. He was wearing a green practice jersey and matching sweat pants, but they weren't nearly as tight as the coach's, which is why he probably didn't look as muscular at the moment.

The two men approached.

"I'm Coach Clifford Montgomery, and this young man is your new quarterback, Karl Johnston," the older man said with a bit of a Southern twang Billy recognized, for they were from the same part of Virginia that he was. "Assistant Coach Frase will run you through your drills today. Which one of you is Greenberg?"

"I am," Billy answered.

"You come with Karl and me," Coach Montgomery said as he signaled for Billy to follow.

As Billy left his teammates, he shrugged his shoulders but did as he was told and caught up with the new coach and quarterback.

"I think it's important that a center and quarterback get to know each other intimately. You two will have to work closer than anyone else on the team, you understand, Greenberg?" the coach asked.

"Yes, sir," Billy responded.

"Good."

Karl just looked back at Billy and smiled.

They continued walking in silence until they reached the locker room, then went back to the room that was usually used for rehabilitation with its massage tables, whirlpool and other useful equipment. Billy noticed the coach had moved some things around and created a large area in the middle of the room with a section of workout mats. Needless to say, Billy was a little confused. After playing football and the same position for over fifteen years, he was used to new coaches, but never had been brought into a situation with just the coach and quarterback.

"I hear you aren't heading for the pros after college? They say you're going to medical school," Coach Montgomery said.

"Yes, sir, I've always wanted to be a doctor. Playing football was a way of getting scholarship money, and what I didn't spend on undergrad, I can use for medical school," Billy answered, expecting the coach to give him the same spiel he always got about how with his talents he should go pro and all.

"Good for you," the coach said, surprising Billy. "You'll have a longer career as a doctor and be able to walk without pain after thirty as well."

"Wow," Billy responded. "You're the first coach to give me that response."

"Johnston here is also pre-med, and the sexy fucker wants to be a surgeon, so I need for you to protect him, so he doesn't injure those hands," Coach Montgomery informed him. "I am not all that keen on playing pro unless you're too stupid to become something else. All that money and a broken body never make for a good combination or a happy long life."

Karl smiled, while Billy wondered if he actually heard the coach call him a 'sexy fucker.' This wouldn't be too shocking, for coaches and players usually referred to each other with sexual innuendoes and pet names all the time. It was a male-bonding thing, yet there was something about how he said it and the fact that Karl smiled and still had not said a word.

"Damn, a surgeon. Cool. I'm going to become an OBGYN," Billy said directly to Karl.

"All that pussy? Can you handle it?" Karl finally spoke, and what a deep, sexy voice he had, Billy thought as he smiled back at his new quarterback.

"OK, enough of this flirting, love birds, let's get to work," the coach said. He then handed Billy a football. "Greenberg, I want you to practice hiking to Johnston. I don't want any fumbles, none. You hear me?"

They both nodded as Billy bent over to hike the ball. The room was particularly hot, and Billy was dressed in all his pads. He was thankful he had not put on his helmet or he would have passed out.

"Aren't you curious what it's on?" Karl asked.

"Oh yeah," Billy said. "It's just that this is strange for me. I've played center for as long as I can remember, and I never had to practice hiking like this in a room away from everyone."

"You'll find I have new ways of doing everything," Coach Montgomery said. "Before we get started, why don't you get out of those pads; it's hot as fuck in here, and I don't want your parents crying to me when you die of heat exhaustion."

Billy turned to leave the room, when the coach stopped him. "Where the hell are you going?"

"To put on some sweats," Billy said.

"Forget the sweats," the coach said. "Just take off the pads. We're all men here. Hell, you've seen parts of your teammates they've never seen themselves every time you girls shower together."

Billy turned around and took off his practice jersey then his shoulder pads. He was wearing a white T-shirt underneath that was soaked with sweat and clinging to every muscular inch of his torso, but he decided to leave it on. He then took off his shoes and his football pants. Now he was just standing there in a jockstrap that did little to contain his huge basket. His teammates had teased him for years about his big balls and thick swinging dick, so he waited for the usual comments. None came. The coach and new quarterback sort of looked but were all business. Billy was grateful.

"On thirty-two," Karl said as Billy bent over once again. Karl placed the back of his hand against Billy's balls and formed a cup with the other facing up, waiting for the ball, and began, "Twelve, sixteen, thirty-two ..." and before he could say hike, Billy had launched the ball between his legs, into Karl's hands and was propelling forward before Karl knew what hit him, dropping the ball.

"They said he was the quickest center ever, Johnston," Coach Montgomery said with a chuckle as Karl picked up the ball. "He's already knocked down three guys, and a fourth is gonna grab that ball ... Coach Phillips already warned me about you, Greenberg."

Billy smiled, but he was not the cocky type, so he felt a little sorry for Karl. "Sorry about that. Let's try it again."

"You're gonna take a little getting used to," Karl said as he wiped some sweat off his brow. "This one on three."

He bent over again, and Karl began, "Seven, four, twenty-two, three ..." and again he dropped the ball as Billy hiked with lightning speed and lurched forward, but this time the coach was standing right in front of him, so he stopped just short of knocking him over.

"Fuck!" Karl said frustrated.

"Greenberg, bend over," the Coach said. "Watch, Johnston." And the coach took the quarterback's position behind Billy. "You gotta slam the back of your hand up there," and he firmly 'slammed' the back of his right hand against Billy's balls, then formed a cup with the other hand below it waiting for the hike. It wasn't enough to hurt, just enough to send a shiver up Billy's spine. "And hold them there. You should place them in just the right position to lift this big sexy ass off the ground." And with that, he lifted Billy off his feet, leaving the center to use the ball as a support to keep from falling flat on his face. The coach then gently put him back down. "That way, no matter when he hikes the ball, you won't drop it. Now you try."

When the coach removed his hands, Billy actually missed them then he realized his dick was starting to swell a bit, and some precum was leaking out. Now, he wished he had gone to get those sweat pants. He hoped that if he continued to sweat as much as he was now, his jock might be too wet for anyone to notice.

"On twenty-three." Karl resumed his position, this time slamming the back of his hand up Billy's crotch, then forming a cup with the other hand. He then attempted to lift Billy up, but he couldn't, so he just began, "Twelve, twenty, sixteen, twenty-three ..." and this time he held onto the ball, but not before almost dropping it again.

"You're getting it ... again," the Coach said.

Billy quickly assumed the position before they could notice the precum or the fact that his dick was starting to grow.

He really wished he could get his sweats.

"On seventeen this time," Karl said. "Wait a minute; it's too fucking hot in here." Then Karl kicked off his shoes, pulled off his sweat pants and removed his shirt, wearing nothing but a jockstrap himself. Billy could see all this when he looked through his legs. Now he knew he was in trouble, for Karl was a brown-skinned god. He then slammed his hand against Billy's balls, but this time he slid them up and down just a tiny bit. "Damn, your butt is all sweaty," Karl complained.

"Just get to it," Coach Montgomery said.

"Thirteen, four, fifty-six, forty-two, forty-three, sixteen, seventeen ..."

Billy hiked and lurched forward, and when he turned around, Karl had the ball firmly in his hand and a big smile on his face. He looked over at the coach who had taken off his shirt, and he really worried about that wet spot on his jock.

"Again," the coach said.

Billy assumed the position for three more hikes. By now, both Billy and Karl were covered in sweat, and he had finally removed his own wet T-shirt. On the fourth try, Billy waited for the familiar 'slam' of Karl's hand, but it didn't come.

Instead, he felt something soft and realized it was Karl's tongue on his ass!

"Oh man, I just couldn't help myself," Karl said between licks. "I couldn't stare at this beautiful butt a minute longer."

Billy looked up and saw the coach's bare feet in front of him. With his hands still on the ball, he looked up, and Coach Montgomery was standing there wearing nothing, not even a jock, and his long thick, dark brown cock was pointing straight out above Billy's head. The coach then squatted down, looked the surprised center in the eyes, and said, "You are one beautiful man." Then, he planted his thick full lips on Billy's, and they made out, swapping spit and encircling each other's tongues. He never took his hands off the ball, and he no longer worried about the wet spot as his jock was one sticky mess with the coach's tongue in his mouth and Karl's all over his ass.

Karl reached up and grabbed the waistband of Billy's jock to pull it off, or at least he tried for the center's dick was so big and hard, it was making it difficult. Karl reached between Billy's thighs and freed the obstruction, giving the sweat and precum coated dick a nice stroking while he removed the jock with the other hand and never letting his tongue leave the hot ass in front of him.

The coach continued to make out with him, and Billy didn't want him to stop, but the coach left the center's mouth for just a second, and replaced his tongue with his long, thick cock. Billy finally let go of the ball and grabbed the backs of Coach Montgomery's thighs.

No one said a word. There were slurps and moans of satisfaction, but nothing needed to be said.

Billy's ass suddenly felt cool as Karl stopped licking it, slid between the center's thighs and flipped over on his back. He then grabbed Billy's butt and pulled him toward him until the center's enormous cock was aiming at his mouth, and Billy did as directed until he felt the warmth of the quarterback's mouth on his dick. But this position didn't quite work, so Karl slid from between his legs, stood and guided Billy over to one of the massage tables. He made Billy lie down on his back. The quarterback then bent over and with easy access gave Billy the wettest, most sensual blowjob of his young life, and it was a good thing he had a wide mouth to accommodate Billy's legendary cock. The coach stood near Billy's head and stuck his cock back into the center's mouth.

Karl was stroking his dick and about to blow, when he announced, "Who wants it?"

"I do," the coach said, and with that he bent over just in time for the quarterback to stroke his cock one more time, aiming it at the coach's mouth. Coach Montgomery then took Karl's dick gladly and swallowed every bit of the young quarterback's tasty load.

"My turn. Take it Greenberg," and the coach blew his huge load into Billy's mouth, which brought him closer to the edge. Billy made sure to get every drop, and the coach did not deny him any.

"Who gets mine?" Billy panted as he let the coach's cock slip from his mouth. Neither the coach nor the quarterback said a word; they just both went down on his throbbing cock, swapping spit between them, and when he shot, one mouth was on it, then the other, and back and forth until he was spent.

The coach looked down at Billy and said, "This is how I like for my center and quarterback to know each other intimately."

FOOTBALL

DADDIES

Dan and Bobby had played football together for close to thirty years, from peewee, through high school and finally on the same pro team and always on the offensive line. When Dan decided before he turned forty-two that it was time to retire, Bobby came to the same conclusion within minutes. He couldn't imagine playing the game without his best friend around, especially since they had been lovers for the past fifteen years. But, they didn't know what to do in retirement? A lot of football players went into the restaurant business or lent their names to other service industry venues, but Dan and Bobby had no interest in that. Their decision became easier when they heard of a gym that was up for sale in their hometown because the owner had died and his kids had no intention of running it.

They flew down to Elkhart, North Carolina, a small town most maps ignore, and made an offer on the old place. The heirs were more than happy to unload the business and accepted their price without hesitation. Dan and Bobby paid cash and found themselves in the gym business.

Once they found a place to rent until they decided where to live permanently, they began the work of renovating what would become the D&B Fitness Factory. This was one of those old-time gyms with benches, free weights, no machines to speak of, and only a couple of stationary bikes serving as cardio equipment. There were mirrors on all the walls and an open shower room that could accommodate eight people at a time.

The work began with getting rid of all the old equipment, so they donated it to an organization that sends fitness gear to developing countries. They ordered all new benches, rubber coated plates, a few basic machines and a couple of treadmills and arc trainers. Their goal was to keep the gym as 'old-school' as possible. They figured if they tried to go fancy, they would not be able to compete with the 'pretty boy' club in the next town.

Elkhart may have been a small town, but football was huge there. Dan and Bobby weren't the only former residents to go pro. Many of their former teammates bought property near the coast, which was only a thirty minute drive from where they were, and once they opened for business, the D&B Fitness Factory filled up every day with quite a few muscle daddies.

Dan and Bobby were all too happy to offer a gym their fellow gray hairs could enjoy. Dan stood over six feet and weighed over 250 pounds of solid muscle with a fifty-inch chest, nineteen-inch arms and maintaining a thirty-six-inch waist, all covered in salt and pepper fur from his head to his feet. Bobby was smooth, but no less impressive with a shaved head to match. He stood barely five-ten, weighed almost 225 pounds, but had just as much muscle as Dan with an even broader chest and bigger biceps, but he carried a few inches around his belly. He had one of those tight bellies that many a boy finds sexy. Dan loved Bobby's belly and would come on it every chance he could get. They were both also hung very nicely and circumcised with big round balls, making for a beautiful sight in the bedroom.

The gym was doing very well as they had tapped into a market that the mega-gyms were ignoring. It also helped that they did not require that their members wear shirts, only proper footwear and shorts as long as they cleaned off the equipment after each use. Dan and Bobby did this mostly for their own entertainment since they both enjoyed watching big men get all sweaty and pumped. Even with the lenient rules, the place was kept immaculate, especially the shower room, which was no small feat considering some of the action rumored to be occurring in there especially before the 10:00 pm closing time.

Dan and Bobby had not engaged in any of the antics but had witnessed a few while they were working. They had hired a college senior, who was getting a degree as a physical therapist, to work the evening hours, so they could have a life outside the business, and he was a very hard worker. Miles was also an offensive lineman in high school, who decided not to play college ball for reasons he never explained, so Bobby and Dan took a special liking to him. At twenty-two years old, Miles was already as big as many of the pros, standing at over six-foot-four and over 260 pounds with a solid frame holding a fifty-two-inch chest and twenty-inch arms. He was not only big and muscular, but he was devastatingly handsome as well with dark features, curly black hair and covered in just a touch of curly black fur. When he smiled, men and women melted regardless of their sexual inclinations.

Dan joked that he didn't care how competent he was; Miles had the job the second he applied. What made him even more appealing was his lack of attitude or ego. Miles was a damn hard worker and kept the gym spotless and in order. He never engaged in 'activities,' nor did he do anything inappropriate. He was quiet and respectful with a pleasant demeanor. He only made one request. Miles wanted to be able to work out after the gym closed for the evening since this would not interfere with his studies. Dan and Bobby suspected Miles was a bit of a loner, for he never received personal calls, was seen texting or had any buddies come by the gym to visit. They wanted to invite him over for dinner, but somehow never got around to it. What they did learn was that his parents died when he was very young and that he was raised by his grandmother, who recently died. He had no other family and lived in the apartment where he was raised.

Dan and Bobby would usually work out mid-day when the gym was the least busy, but this became a hassle as the business of running a business takes more time than people realize, so they decided to try working out at 4:00 am before they opened. This lasted only a couple of days because getting up at 3:00 am was nearly impossible, too. That was when Dan suggested they follow Miles's lead and work out after hours. This would work since they hired Bobby's nephew to open for them during the week, and they could come in around 7:00 am. Bobby's nephew was competent but not worth the trouble of describing since he spent most of his time at work surfing the net and texting his girlfriend. He was just there to occupy space until Dan and Bobby came in. Miles left the place in such order that there was nothing to do in the mornings, and Bobby told Miles that he knew his nephew was useless, but he needed him for those two hours, so he and Dan could get some rest. Miles never complained. And, Dan and Bobby would keep the place in order while they worked and tended to the business as well.

Around 10:30 pm, Dan and Bobby showed up on the first night they decided to try their new workout schedule. The gym was closed, and the blinds were drawn indicating it was closed, but they could see Miles's shadow as he worked out inside. They told Miles they would be coming in to work out, so that he wouldn't be startled when the door opened.

Dan and Bobby walked in just as Miles lay down on a bench to perform dumbbell presses with 110-pound weights. They both stopped in their tracks at the sight before them. Wearing nothing but a pair of black 2xist briefs that did little to hide his candy and a pair of New Balance cross trainers, he was pushing the weights up, and his chest was glistening and pumped.

He finished his set and sat up on the bench. "Hey, when you didn't show up at closing, I decided to get comfortable. I'll go get my shorts," Miles said as he greeted them.

"Don't ...," Dan almost shouted.

"... worry about us," Bobby interrupted. "Stay comfortable."

"Are you sure?" Miles asked as he stood up, revealing his body to them for the first time.

"I didn't realize how hot it gets in here with the AC off. Why didn't you reprogram it to stay on for an hour after closing?" Bobby asked.

"I didn't think I had the authority," Miles the ever-dutiful employee responded. "Besides, I prefer it warm when I work out."

Dan and Bobby walked toward the locker room to put away their gym bags, and Miles dropped to the floor to do a set of push-ups. They each glanced at his perfect, big and muscular butt as it went up and down.

In the locker room, Dan took off his shirt as Bobby did the same. "Should we strip down as well?" Dan whispered.

"I might pop wood," Bobby said with a smile. "But, what the hell?!?"

They each stripped down, Dan to a pair of white Calvin Klein briefs, and Bobby to a pair of black trunk briefs of the same brand. They exited the locker room and joined Miles in the gym. Miles went about his chest work out as if everything was normal, and Dan and Bobby did the same while they worked legs.

Occasionally, they would smile at each other, but Miles was very serious about his workouts, as were Dan and Bobby, and after the initial excitement of being half naked with the college senior wore off, all were grunting and sweating their asses off.

Miles was attempting to do a set of incline dumbbell presses with 100-pound weights, but was struggling to lift them into position to begin his set. Dan noticed this and offered to help him.

"Thanks, maybe I should begin with these. I can never lift them up this far into my workout," Miles said as Dan walked over. Bobby followed.

"Lie back; Bobby and I'll hand them to you."

"I'll give you a spot, once you get started," Bobby added.

Miles lay back, and Dan and Bobby on either side of him lifted up the dumbbells and waited until Miles was holding them firmly. Bobby then positioned himself behind Miles to spot him. He managed five reps before he needed assistance, and Bobby helped him with two more.

Once he was done with the set, Miles thanked them, but Bobby remained crouched behind the bench. Dan looked at him, and Bobby motioned downward with his eyes, for he was sporting a hard-on that could not be hidden.

"Let us know when you are ready for another set," Dan said and winked at Bobby.

Miles lay down on the bench again, and was ready in thirty seconds. The kid really did an intense workout.

They helped him get a grip on the dumbbells again, and Bobby hoped Miles didn't see the bulge in his trunk briefs.

Miles did this set and another, and at that point, Bobby's underwear was soaked with precum. He quickly went to the locker room to fetch another pair he hoped he remembered to put in his gym bag. There was a pair, and by the time he had removed the soaked pair and wiped off his dick, he was no longer as hard, but still a little firm. He changed into a matching pair of black trunk briefs, which was a relief, for he would have to explain the change in wardrobe.

He exited the locker room and the sight he saw was about to ruin another pair of underwear. Dan was doing a set of squats, and Miles was spotting him from behind. Bobby stood there awestruck at the sight before him, and his dick was now out of control, hard as a rock and leaking like a faucet. When Dan struggled for a few more reps, Miles leaned in closely to help. Two reps later, the set was done.

Miles stepped back, and Dan stepped away from the rack, and he was now sporting a rager equal to Bobby's. He looked over at Bobby, who looked over at Miles, who looked at both of them and smiled.

"I get hard when I work out, too," Miles said. And when they looked down, they noticed his underwear was beginning to stretch quite a bit. He then dropped down and did another set of push-ups, while Dan and Bobby watched.

Dan looked at Bobby and shrugged, and Bobby shrugged back. Miles then finished his set and declared his workout was done, and he was going to take a shower. Meanwhile, the bulge in his briefs was bigger than before and the head of his dick was sticking out of the waistband. Miles walked past Bobby and into the locker room. Within seconds, the sound of a shower being turned on was heard, and Bobby turned to follow him.

"Are we done working out?" Dan asked as he followed Bobby.

Bobby never answered. He stepped out of his newly precummed briefs and into the shower room where Miles was using the middle-most showerhead. Dan followed suit. Bobby chose the shower to the right of Miles and Dan decided to occupy the one on the left. They watched as Miles soaped himself up and were mesmerized by his pumped, heavily muscled and lathered body and his enormous circumcised cock that stood out and up. Dan and Bobby's not quite as big, but big enough dicks were just as hard.

Dan soaped himself up waiting for Bobby to take the lead if anything were going to happen. And, take the lead Bobby did. He lathered up his hand, reached down, and began stroking Miles's dick, and he was met with no resistance. Dan then leaned in and kissed Bobby full on the mouth, and their tongues wrestled as Miles reached down and stroked both their cocks. Within seconds, Bobby was ready to pop, so he grabbed Miles's hand to stop the momentum, but Miles proved to be quite strong. That strength was all it took, and Bobby was shouting and shooting a load all over Miles's hand and leg.

Not even a second after that, Dan added to the spunk on Miles and shouted his pleasure as well. The hands of a physical therapist were obviously magic. Dan planted his mouth back on Miles and Bobby continued to stroke the enormous cock until it shot a load all over the shower wall – a load so impressive that Dan and Bobby almost applauded.

Once he caught his breath, Miles declared, "I've never touched a man before. I have wanted to do that with you guys since the day you hired me."

"You never touched a man?" Bobby asked with surprise.

"Where did you learn to stroke like that?" Dan asked.

"I guess from playing with myself," Miles said as he resumed soaping himself up.

Bobby stopped him, and Dan joined Bobby as they lathered up Miles, taking turns kissing him and stroking him until he shot another load – this time on the shower floor.

# # # # #

Dan and Bobby soon found a 19th Century home that suited them perfectly and settle in nicely. Miles graduated from college and landed a job at a local hospital as a physical therapist.

Does Miles still work at the gym part-time? You bet he does, and he still works out in his underwear after closing every night along with Dan and Bobby. But now, they sometimes shower at the gym or the three of them go home afterward to shower, where they live in a polyamorous relationship that has 'worked out' quite well.

Teammates for life!

KOSHER MAN GETS PORKED

Mordecai arrived home, flying in through the window (how no one ever saw him arrive home that way every night was mystery) after a long night, mainly dealing with gang-related violence. Somehow, the AN66 gang found its way to Greenberg, and they were wreaking havoc on the citizens of this fine metropolis. Our hero was both exhausted and exhilarated as his moonlighting activities usually had that effect on him.

He stripped off his tights and walked into the bathroom. As he turned on the shower and tested the water temperature, he looked down just as his kosher cock started to rise. He stepped into the shower, and no sooner had he reached for the soap, when his member was at its full twelve-by-seven attention. Mordecai wrapped a soapy hand around the huge appendage and with just a few strokes shot a load that reached up to his chin. The shower rinsed it away before he could scoop it up for a taste. As usual, it had been months since he had sex, and with each passing day, it took less and less time to come as he was hornier than a Bonobo monkey.

Mordecai climbed into bed and looked at the clock – 3:00 am – meaning he would barely get four hours sleep before heading to work at the museum. He dozed quickly.

"Help!" someone screamed from a good distance away. "Help!" he screamed again.

Mordecai sat up.

"Help!" the man screamed again.

He strained to determine the direction of the scream. When he did, he jumped out of bed and, in a flash, transformed into Kosher Man. He jumped through the window, and the sound of breaking glass reminded him that once again he forgot to open it.

"Now, I know somebody had to have heard that," he said out loud as he flew in the direction of the man's screams. "And, my landlord must be suspicious about all the broken windows."

He located the man in distress; he was standing in the middle of a dark alley.

"Why are they always standing in a dark alley? Wouldn't it be smarter to go out to the street and call the police, so I can get some sleep?"

Mordecai landed in a flourish, and his cape temporarily covered his head before he grabbed it and straightened it out.

"Are you OK?"

"I am now that you are here, Kosher Man."

Our hero stepped forward to help, but he noticed something that made him suspicious. The man's hair looked like a wig. He reached up to the man and grabbed the wig, and just as he thought, there was a swastika tattooed on his skull.

"You are an AN66 member!" Kosher Man yelled, but before he could grab the hoodlum, a vat above his head flipped over, and before he knew it, he was covered in a hot, white creamy liquid that had lumps and smelled like soup.

Almost immediately, Kosher Man slumped to the ground, for it wasn't the heat that affected him, but the soup's main ingredient – clams, which had grazed his lips as the soup cascaded down. He had been doused with New England clam chowder. "TREYF!" he yelled. (For those of the Gentile persuasion, *treyf* is non-kosher food.)

As he lay there writhing in pain, more AN66 members, all with shaved heads, swastika skull tattoos and dressed identically in jack boots, tan pants and leather jackets appeared.

"Grab the kike," one who appeared to be the leader yelled, and several of them picked up Kosher

Man, straining to lift him up over their heads and carried him away.

Kosher Man awoke several hours later and found himself in a sling, his hands tied above his head with pork sausage, and his legs tied separately with the same vile ingredient. He was stripped naked, except for his mask, as even villains never remove a superhero's mask when they capture him, which remains one of life's great mysteries.

Whereas under normal circumstances and tied in the same fashion without the use of pork sausage, he would have been turned on and probably sporting a massive hard-on, his dick hung limply, and he was in excruciating pain.

He also knew that if he remained like this for too long he would die, for pork (and other *treyf*) was his Kryptonite.

The AN66 leader walked over to him and looked down at the dying hero with a smile that more resembled a grimace.

"Before long, you Jew bastard, we will be rid of you, and we'll rule this town." He then tried to laugh maniacally, but he was not that good of an actor, which Kosher Man mentally noted as he was unable to speak.

"Get the tenderloin," the wannabe supervillain barked at his charges.

Three of the AN66s brought a large slab of meat over to where our hunky hero was slung up and held it up to his exposed anus.

If that is a pork tenderloin, I am a dead man, he thought as he braced himself for the assault.

"I figured pork would be your downfall, Jewboy," the not even B-movie worthy actor/leader said to Kosher Man as he signaled for his flunkies to shove the pork tenderloin up his ass.

They aimed, and just as they got about eight inches of it up his hole, a loud commotion was heard outside the dungeon. There were loud crashes and bangs, cracking and yelling, slumping and dragging, kapowing and moaning. Then, the door burst open, and a tall, muscular man in beige tights with little black dots all over them and a matching mask and cape leapt into the room, followed by a smaller, but no less muscular man, wearing beige tights that were not adorned with the black dots but appeared light and fluffy, nonetheless.

"Who the fuck are you?" the AN66 leader yelled.

"I am Matzo Man, and this is my sidekick, Matzo Ball," he answered as they proceeded to kick ass all over the dungeon, eventually tying up the leader and the three men who were porking Kosher Man.

The two newly arrived superheroes then raced over to the sling and quickly untied the pork sausage restraints. They both looked down and saw the remainder of the pork tenderloin hanging out our hero's *tuchus*, and they pulled it out so quickly, that his sphincter popped.

"Aunt Rose, get in here," Matzo Man yelled to the outer hallway.

Kosher Man's mother then entered the room and immediately opened her purse and pulled out a syringe. "What did they do to him?"

"They rammed a pork tenderloin up his *tuchus*," Matzo Ball said.

"MB, she's a lady," Matzo Man said to his sidekick.

"That's quite all right," Rose said as she prepared the antidote and filled the syringe. She plunged the needle into her son's chest, and he coughed before opening his eyes.

He then closed his eyes, for he thought he was hallucinating. He opened them again, looked at the two beige rescuers and asked, "Who are you?"

"Mordecai, you don't remember your Hebrew school friend, Bernie? And, this is his partner, Morty," Rose said. "I knew you were in trouble, so I called them on the Yenta Line."

"Bernie and Morty?" he asked.

"Bernie is Harvey and Sheila's son. He is also Matzo Man, and Morty is Matzo Ball," she said as if anyone knew that, while she placed the syringe and other items back into her purse.

"We better get him out of here before the police arrive," Bernie, aka Matzo Man, said as he and Morty, aka Matzo Ball, lifted Mordecai, aka Kosher Man, out of the sling. "Where are his tights?"

"Never mind his tights. Get him home and give him three enemas and a hot *Silkwood* shower. The Manischewitz Blackberry won't take full effect until all traces of pork are out of his system," Rose ordered as she left the dungeon.

"Manischewitz Blackberry?" Matzo Ball asked.

"The woman is amazing. She knows just the right wine to serve with *treyf*," Matzo Man said with a wink.

Once back in his apartment, Mordecai was treated to three extreme enemas by his superhero comrades, and he was starting to feel better.

"Now for your hot shower," Bernie, who had stripped down to his briefs, announced as he grabbed one arm and draped it over his shoulder. Morty, who had also stripped out of his costume, grabbed the other arm.

They propped Mordecai up in the tub and turned on the water. As Bernie grabbed the handheld shower and rinsed the hunky hero from head to toe, Morty grabbed a bar of kosher soap.

"You should take off your underwear and get in there with him. It will be easier that way," Bernie said.

Morty, always the loyal partner and sidekick, did as ordered. He was slightly shorter than Bernie's five-ten, but with a thickly muscled, hairy body and a nice thick eight-inch dick with a mushroom head, he was just as sexy. He stepped into the tub and soaped up Mordecai. "He has an incredible body," he swooned as he worked both his patient and himself into a lather, sporting a hard-on in seconds.

"He also has a huge dick," Bernie said as he pointed the shower head at the now rising cock. Bernie then stripped off his briefs revealing his nine inches of thick kosher meat. All the penises were beautiful as a *moyel* does a much better job circumcising than a doctor – even a nice Jewish one.

Although Mordecai had not said much since they arrived home and had endured the invasive enemas, he had a smile across his face as his comrades in tights both cleaned and scrubbed his body of any remnants of the pork that almost killed him.

Morty then eased Mordecai over so that his butt was totally exposed, and he grabbed the showerhead from Bernie, so he could rinse the soap from the big muscular *tuchus*.

"Sweet," Morty said as he looked at the luscious mounds. He just couldn't help himself as he pressed his raging hard cock against the opening that had been through so much abuse only hours earlier. "I want to plow that so badly."

"Don't do it badly, do it right," Mordecai said, finally uttering a complete sentence for the first time since being doused with New England clam chowder. Mordecai, who was a bit of a neat freak – and anal retentive, usually wouldn't dream of being topped, but the hunky sidekick with the big Hebrew National and his freshly cleaned colon made for a perfect opportunity. And, Mordecai was not one to pass up a good opportunity.

"And, you," Mordecai said to Bernie, "feed me that cock of yours," for this was the rarest of good opportunities.

It didn't take long for Mordecai to be getting it from both ends like a nice brisket on a rotisserie. With the hot water cascading down on them, they fucked and sucked until the walls shook.

Morty rarely topped and this was a treat worth more than anything he would get during the eight nights of Hanukah. For Mordecai, who rarely got laid, this was heaven on earth.

He also struggled to remember the Hebrew prayer thanking God for good sex.

His own cock was hard and throbbing although he had not touched it as his hands were all over Bernie's *tuchus* while he swallowed every inch of his kosher meat. The copious precum made it all the more pleasurable, and Mordecai didn't fear any remnants or *treyf* coming from this treat.

There were moans and groans, cries of "Oh God," and lots of heavy breathing.

Bernie came first, filling Mordecai's mouth with a kosher protein shake, which he swallowed like a superhero. Bernie immediately dove between Mordecai's legs and stretched his mouth over the foot-long bull cock that was leaking buckets of precum just in time to taste and swallow Mordecai's load, which shot without so much as any handy work, for Morty was fucking him in the most glorious manner, both strong and gentle at the same time, massaging his prostate perfectly. The spasms from his anus drained a load from Morty, who filled Mordecai's guts with his own kosher protein shake as he yelled, "Hallelujah!"

After cleaning each other off, Bernie and Morty stayed the night with Mordecai, sleeping on either side of him – an additional treat for our lonely superhero, who always slept alone.

The next morning, after bagels and lox, they returned to their own metropolis, Mogen David City. But before they left, they promised to come and visit Mordecai at least once a month, and he promised he would do the same and smiled as he waved goodbye, and they drove off in their brown 1976 Eldorado convertible.

"All we need is a female superhero, and we can form the Jewish Justice League of America," Mordecai said to himself as he walked back upstairs to his apartment.

When he entered, his phone rang.

"Hello?"

"So, *nu*?" his mother asked.

SELFISH PRICK

Start from the beginning; tell me what happened.

How far back do you want me to go?

How far back do you need to go?

Considering yesterday was the first time I saw Paul Tucker since 1989, maybe 21 years?

You had not seen him since 1989?

That's right.

And, you were expecting to see him here, yesterday?

In Missoula, Montana? I had no idea he was here. Last I heard he was in San Diego.

Paul Tucker has not lived in San Diego in over a decade.

How the hell was I supposed to know that? As I said the last time I saw him was 1989.

But, you had spoken to him?

No.

You had not spoken to him or seen him since 1989, and yesterday, he just shows up at your hotel room – out of the blue?

I had heard from him ... twice.

Twice?

Twice.

Start from the beginning.

Picture it, Norfolk, Virginia, 1989 ...

Don't be cute, Mr. Sagman.

Whatever you say, Detective Anthony.

Go on.

There was a bar in Norfolk, which may still be there. I don't know as I have not lived there since 1992. It was called the Late Show. It was a member's only, after hours bar. At least it was advertised as member's only, but just about anyone could get in.

I used to go there every Friday night because I worked as a waiter in Williamsburg, lived in Newport News, and I had to be at work at 5:00 am on Sunday mornings, so Friday was my day to go out. And, every Friday, I was at the Late Show.

What kind of bar was this?

As I said, an afterhours member's only bar.

You know what I mean.

A gay bar ... any way, one night, and I don't remember when, I met two guys, one was in the Air Force and one was in the Navy ...

You said this was a gay bar.

Yeah, and Norfolk as well as all of Hampton Roads is full of military guys, and guess what? They go to gay bars – every closeted one of them. When the first Gulf War broke out, the bars emptied out like a restaurant when the immigration officer shows up.

Was one of these men Paul Tucker?

Yes, he was in the Navy then. I don't remember the name of the Air Force guy. Funny thing is, the Air Force guy wanted to go home with me, but I wanted to go home with Paul.

Are you aware that Paul Tucker was married?

I found out later, but you'll have to wait for that part. Also, he wasn't married then. He was single and living the gay life ... so to speak.

So to speak?

Are you going to let me finish?

Go on.

I told the Air Force guy ... I wish I could remember his name ... that I was tired. I gave my number to both of them and said we should get together for a movie or something sometime. A couple of days, or the next day, again I can't remember, Paul calls me, and we go out hiking. I remember it was a Sunday afternoon, and we were out for quite some time.

I noticed from the beginning that he wasn't quite happy, and he hid his unhappiness by pointing out how unhappy I was. Funny thing is I always considered myself happy, so I didn't know how to take this guy telling me I couldn't possibly be happy.

Anyway, we came back to my apartment. I was living in Newport News then, and we ended up in bed together. He had a cute body, but the truth is he was quite boring in bed. He liked showering together, and he was shaved from head to toe. I asked him how he did that in the barracks without raising suspicion, and he said his bunkmate or roommate or whatever they call them thought it was cool and did it himself.

So, we dated for a couple of weeks, and he would spend the night some times. He also wore a fake wedding ring when he was out in public with me. One morning, a co-worker stopped by to borrow some money for an alternator or battery, and he was sitting at my dining table shirtless, so he flashed the wedding ring, so she wouldn't think he was my gay boyfriend who just spent the night.

I just looked at him as if he were retarded and asked what else she would think of a shirtless guy sitting at my table at 8:00 am.

After a couple of weeks of this relationship, if you want to call it that, he sends me a letter telling me he doesn't want to see me again. He says I, meaning me, could never be happy, and he could never be happy with me because sleeping with me was the equivalent of jerking off. I remember that. I never responded and chalked it up to one bad experience. I also vowed never to date another Navy guy.

Did you hear from him again?

Not exactly. I ran into our mutual Air Force acquaintance a few weeks later and he gave me the scoop. Apparently, Mr. Tucker was a conflicted sort. He was once an exchange student to Bolivia, and he was sent home for having sex with another boy. I know from being an AFS sponsor ...

AFS?

American Field Service.

Oh.

That having sex with anyone, gay or straight, was a no-no. He also told me Paul had a difficult relationship with his father. Who doesn't? Again, I really didn't care. Boo hoo, cry me a river, move on. That is how I felt.

And that was it? You weren't angry? You didn't feel the need to exact revenge?

Why would I exact revenge? I should use that in my next book.

You won't have a next book if we find you did this.

Please, Detective Anthony. If I exacted revenge on every guy who rejected me, there would be trail of bodies up and down the Eastern Seaboard.

Oh, I doubt you even understand rejection, Mr. Sagman. You have those movie star looks, the body of an Adonis, and the fake charm to go with it.

Are you hitting on me?

Hardly.

Well, what you ordinary people don't understand is people like me ... and I know what I look like ... get rejected all the time. You see, we may turn heads when we walk into a room, and we may be the object of someone's obsessive pursuits, but once they get us in bed and find out we're really nice guys, they do everything in their power to make us feel bad about ourselves before they move on.

You just gave us motive.

As I said, I have better things to do than murder someone. I am a best-selling author; two of my books are being made into movies – simultaneously. Do you really think I would risk going to jail by murdering some selfish prick who rejected me twenty-one years ago?

That is what I am trying to find out. So when was the next time you saw Mr. Tucker.

Yesterday.

OK. Talked to him?

Yesterday.

Did you know he was living in Missoula?

I knew he was from Montana, but I never knew what city. I figured Helena or Butte.

Did you know he just moved here less than a year ago?

Not until yesterday.

So, you didn't know that he lived near Baltimore ... an hour away from you in Rockville for almost five years?

Actually it was Tolson, and not until yesterday when he told me. He also told me he lived in Oklahoma as well. And, Baltimore is only forty-five minutes away.

You never heard from him in twenty-one years?

I didn't say that. I said, I never spoke to him or saw him in twenty-one years. You're trying to trip me up.

I'm just trying to get to the truth, Mr. Sagman.

So, Detective Anthony. Are you good cop or bad cop?

You watch too much television.

I have written a few episodes of crime dramas, and this experience should help me.

You may be writing them in a cell.

I doubt that. I didn't murder Paul Tucker.

Some people think you did.

And, those people are wrong.

So, when did you hear from him again?

I'm not exactly sure, but I think it was 1994 or 1995 ... or was it 1996. My father called me to tell me that someone sent me a letter to their address because he couldn't find me. So, he forwarded the letter to me. I was living in West Palm Beach.

Florida?

Yeah. The letter was from Paul. There was a photograph of him with a woman. And, the letter pretty much told me that he had found God while taking a walk or stroll and found true happiness and married this woman named Lori. And, in typical Paul Tucker fashion, he proceeded to tell me that he hoped I could one day be happy and blah blah blah ...

How did that make you feel?

What, you're now a therapist?

Mr. Sagman, I don't think you understand the seriousness of this. A man was shot twice and killed in your hotel room, and you were the last one to see him alive.

Believe me, I understand the seriousness, and I understand the ridiculousness of this.

Go on.

How did the letter make me feel? At first I was disturbed, and then I felt sorry for his wife. I predicted then and there that after ten years, she would catch him with a man or he would eventually come out after not having sex with her for a long time. And, I was angry at him. Not for what he did to me. I had long forgotten about that, and as I said earlier, never cared. I was angry because here was another gay man, using a woman to find happiness and fucking with her emotions, not to mention her life. I wondered how much he told her. Was this part of some ex-gay ministry and she was a former lesbian? If so, then more power to them. But, if he married her without being open and honest, what a selfish prick.

You were angry?

At the situation.

That is the second time you've called him a selfish prick.

He was one.

You were angry at him.

OK, I was angry. You want to know why? This guy dumps me, sends me a letter telling me I could never be happy, tells me that sex with me is like jerking off, then marries a woman, sends me this smiling bullshit picture, and again tells me I am not happy. I haven't seen this selfish prick in five or so years, and he assumes I am not happy. Who the fuck is he? Seriously, who the fuck is he?

So, you killed him.

Please. He would not be worth the energy. I was angry for a minute, then I forgot about it.

Did you respond to the letter?

Fuck no. I didn't want anything to do with him.

So, that's it? Then yesterday you see him again.

There was another letter?

Really?

Yes.

When?

I moved to DC in 1997. And, I think a few months after that another letter came via my parents. There's your proof I never responded. He would have known where I lived.

Unless you told him you moved to DC?

No ... I didn't.

What was in the letter?

It was a picture of him running a marathon – shirtless. In it, he said something like, I hope you are happy. My life is wonderful.

And, did you respond?

No. I was dumbfounded. Why would he send me this picture? Shirtless no less? Wasn't he married to a woman? I threw it out. End of story. The guy had no effect on me.

And the next time he contacted you?

Never again.

Until yesterday.

At the book signing. He was about halfway through the line. I recognized him immediately.

Was he alone.

No ... he was standing there right in front of me with his lover ... male lover ... and his son ... his twelve-year-old son.

Were you in shock?

I'd be lying if I said I wasn't.

Who else did you expect to find in Missoula?

I had no idea he lived here. However, my predictions came true. He introduced me to his partner, Mark, and his son, Harry. Mark was all smiles, but Harry. I looked into that boy's eyes, and I saw nothing. No soul. Nothing. It was also clear that Mark had no idea who I was. Paul told him I was an old friend from his days in Virginia. Old friend. We were never friends. But in those fifteen seconds, I figured it all out. His life was one big lie. He never told his wife about his past, and as far as smiling Mark was concerned, Paul's first sexual experience was with him. But, the boy? I will never forget the look on the boy's face.

So, what happened next?

I signed his book, told him it was nice to see him and meet his family and that I couldn't chat because we had to keep the line moving.

Did you tell him where you were staying?

No.

Then how did he find your hotel room?

Come on Detective Anthony. How hard can it be to find out where a minor celebrity is staying in Missoula? Besides, I didn't want to see him. The man means, I mean, meant nothing to me.

What happened next?

The signing was over around five o'clock. I went back to the hotel to shower and change, and my publicist and I had dinner in the hotel restaurant around six. After that, I went back to my room to watch some television and relax.

Where was the gun?

What gun? I have never owned a gun in my life. This is my first time in Missoula. I came off a plane, went straight to the hotel, checked in, then to the book store, then back to the hotel, dinner and back to my room. I carried on my luggage, so I wouldn't take a chance on it being lost. Do you really think I carried a gun on the plane with the intention of killing someone I had no idea was living here? Be real.

You had time to buy one.

Where? I didn't even rent a car. I have never bought, nor handled, nor shot, nor touched a gun in my life.

You expect me to believe that?

Believe what you want.

Why haven't you asked for a lawyer?

I didn't do anything wrong. Besides, my lawyer is in New York, and he is on his way.

Did he tell you not to talk?

Yes, but I have nothing to hide.

Fair enough. When did you invite Paul to your room?

I didn't invite him. He showed up. Around ten, there was a knock on my door. I peeped through the hole, and who is standing there? Paul Tucker.

How did he find your room?

Seriously? You are asking me that again?

OK. What happened next?

I opened the door and asked him what he wanted. He said he wanted to talk. I said I had nothing to say, and he should go home to his happy family and leave me alone because I could never be happy.

So, you were angry.

No, I was being a smart ass. He insisted, so I let him in, but I told him he had ten minutes to talk and that would be it. So, he talked.

What did you talk about?

Not what I thought we would. I honestly thought he would apologize for trying to make me feel less than human all those years ago, but then I realized an apology wouldn't matter anyway. None of us are the same person we were twenty years ago. Instead, he proceeded to tell me what a wonderful life he had and how happy he was, and how happy he wished I could be. Oh my God, it was the same bullshit. This selfish prick, who destroyed so many lives with his need to be so-called normal, was still the same asshole. At that moment, I felt sorry for his partner, his ex-wife, and especially, the kid. Now, I know why that kid looked so … I don't know … soul-less. I mean gay or straight, he was so convinced that nobody else was happy and only by creating a pseudo-happy existence and rubbing everyone else's nose in it could he be happy.

Did you tell him that?

No. I told him I needed a soda. I left the room to go to the vending machine down the hall. When I came back, there he was. Sitting in the chair with blood coming from his crotch and a hole in his forehead, and his brains all over the back of the chair and the wall behind that.

What did you do next?

I called you guys. Or at least I tried. My 911 on my cell phone wouldn't work, and I didn't want to touch anything in the room, so I ran downstairs and had the night manager call you.

That's pretty incredible. You leave to get a soda, and conveniently, he gets murdered in those five minutes. Where did you hide the gun?

Again with the fucking gun.

Who else would have known he was there, Mr. Sagman?

Maybe someone followed him and waited for me to leave the room.

How did that person get in the room?

Well, I never took my key or locked the door when I went to get the soda. I figured Paul for a lot of things, but a thief was never one of them.

Are you sorry he's dead?

No. Why should I be? I am indifferent. I couldn't care less. But, I didn't kill him.

Then, who did, Mr. Sagman? No one else had motive. No one else had opportunity.

Now, who should watch more crime dramas? First, I didn't have motive. I didn't know he lived here. I didn't have opportunity. Besides, where in the fuck would I get a gun? As I said, I have never shot a gun. I have never owned a gun. I have never been to Missoula in my life, and I didn't know the selfish prick lived here. But, I can think of three people who had motive ... and opportunity.

Humor me.

The ex-wife for obvious reasons. The smiling partner because I represented Paul's pre-straight-marital past – a past it would only take a moron not to figure out – and that would just ruin their picture-perfect existence. Imagine a famous writer knowing the real Paul.

Sure, he'd frame the writer. The problem with this theory is I didn't know how either one could have known he was going to pay me a visit until I gave it more thought.

You see people like Paul make my favorite subjects for my books. They live a double existence. On the outside, they are so moral and just, but they have a side that is just as skeevy as everyone else out there. They think they have everyone fooled, but they don't. And, do you know how I know these people so well?

How?

My mother was one of them. She thought she had everyone fooled. She fooled no one. So, my guess is he had visited a lot of people from his past. A guy like Paul leaves a trail that is hard to cover up. I wasn't the first guy he visited in a hotel room. Or, the only guy he sent letters to over the years. I wasn't the only guy he tried to belittle. But, none of us would have the inclination or the desire to kill him. To us, he wasn't worth it. The wife, I'm not so sure. She had motive, but did she want her son to grow up without a father? And, the smiling partner? Murder would have ruined their perfect life. If anything, he would have murdered me.

Then who does that leave, Mr. Sagman? You?

Not me. Have you questioned the son?

How would a twelve-year-old pull something like this off?

Very easily. No one would pay attention to a kid going into a hotel and entering a room. Besides, don't all your kids out here have guns?

Someone would have noticed the kid.

I'm through talking.

Detective?

What, Baker?

You're going to need to let Sagman go.

Why?

The kid confessed.

I'll send you and your wife tickets to the premiere – both of them, Detective Anthony. Now, if you'll excuse me, I have plane to catch.

ABOUT THE AUTHOR

Residing in Rockville, MD, with his rescue beagle, Esmeralda Stern, Milton Stern is a writer, volunteer, and antique car collector. You can read more at www.miltonstern.com.

aring any underwear. "Excuse me," I said, having a hard time loo

linded by that bulge in his crotch, "but don't I know you?" "Mayb

ind of t   bout

with Ra   God,

t loser?   in?" l

iid. "Lik   s stror

ce body   e on (

lly, he l   I eve

ı up to t   any id

staking   ie san

ı, I coul   ery lo

ood raci   ie sw

ng with   e in s

we go (behir

ill see 1   in pu

ed?" he   vent t

rivacy.   grabl

hard. I

k, traci   t, so

ed it, ha

with m   bing

bbing, I   n cocl

LOOKING FOR

MORE HOT STORIES?

WOULD **YOU** LIKE TO **CONTRIBUTE**
TO AN **UPCOMING ANTHOLOGY?**

VISIT

http://www.STARbooksPress.com

Hot Deals!

Subscribe to Our FREE E-mail Newsletter!

Submission Guidelines for Authors!

Buy Books and E-books Online!

VISIT

http://www.STARbooksPress.com

TODAY!

ie sound of unzipping filled the small space. I don't know who's h

but before I knew it, I had his rod in my hand, and mine was in hi

it to do?" he asked, his tone challenging. I knew exactly, and sank

HOTHOUSE BACKROOM
.COM

Join today and get instant access to:

1st Run Hot House Movies

Backroom Exclusive Videos

100s of Hot House Scenes

Free BelAmi Bonus Content

Thousands of XXX Hardcore Pictures

Premium Member Discounts on DVDs

Hot House Exclusive
TONY MECELLI

www.ingramcontent.com/pod-product-compliance
Lightning Source LLC
Chambersburg PA
CBHW031119030726
47496CB00002BA/606